All I wanted to do was s
novels while Blake sat acro
at *Pop Goes the Culture*, his epic tome on twentieth century culture and counter-culture and its influences on the media. Or vice versa. It was a real chicken-and-egg sort of thing as far as I was concerned, even if it was my husband's passion. Anyway, dead bodies weren't part of our empty nest blueprint.

Books by Lois Winston

Anastasia Pollack Crafting Mystery series
Assault with a Deadly Glue Gun
Death by Killer Mop Doll
Revenge of the Crafty Corpse
Decoupage Can Be Deadly
A Stitch to Die For
Scrapbook of Murder
Drop Dead Ornaments
Handmade Ho-Ho Homicide
A Sew Deadly Cruise
Stitch, Bake, Die!
Guilty as Framed

Anastasia Pollack Crafting Mini-Mysteries
Crewel Intentions
Mosaic Mayhem
Patchwork Peril
Crafty Crimes (all 3 novellas in one volume)

Empty Nest Mystery Series
Definitely Dead
Literally Dead

Romantic Suspense
Love, Lies and a Double Shot of Deception
Lost in Manhattan (writing as Emma Carlyle)
Someone to Watch Over Me (writing as Emma Carlyle)

Romance and Chick Lit
Talk Gertie to Me
Four Uncles and a Wedding (writing as Emma Carlyle)
Hooking Mr. Right (writing as Emma Carlyle)
Finding Hope (Writing as Emma Carlyle)

Novellas and Novelettes
Elementary, My Dear Gertie
Moms in Black, A Mom Squad Caper
Once Upon a Romance
Finding Mr. Right

Children's Chapter Book
The Magic Paintbrush

Nonfiction
Top Ten Reasons Your Novel is Rejected
House Unauthorized
Bake, Love, Write
We'd Rather Be Writing

Definitely Dead

LOIS WINSTON

Cover design by L. Winston

ISBN-13: 978-1-940795-09-6

DEDICATION

This one is for my dear friend and cheerleader Janice Boot

ACKNOWLEDGMENTS

Enormous thanks to authors Donnell Bell and Irene Peterson for their critiquing and editing skills and to Mary V. Welk for her medical expertise.

And to my husband Rob who continues to save my sanity when my computer programs are driving me crazy.

ONE

"Is he dead?" As I forced the words out around the hand I'd firmly clamped over my mouth to stifle a gag reflex, I inched away from the body sprawled at my feet. The blood pooling beneath Client Number Thirteen, one Mr. Sidney Mandelbaum, followed me, creeping along the asphalt like some B-movie sinister slime out to get me. *Euw!* I jumped to my left to avoid contact.

Blake crouched into a catcher's position, felt for a pulse, and nodded. "Definitely dead."

I backed up another step. "You're sure?"

"Bashed-in skull. Knife sticking out of his heart." He turned his head and spoke to me over his shoulder. I noticed his skin had taken on a slightly green tinge, but maybe that was a trick of the halogen lights that had switched on to illuminate the twilight-bathed parking lot. Or maybe it was a reflection of my own queasiness. "Yeah, Gracie, I'm sure."

Green tinge not withstanding, both Blake's eyes and the quirky slant of his mouth conveyed *The Look*, the one he saves exclusively for me. And just so there wasn't any doubt in my mind, *The Voice* accompanied *The Look*.

When I met Blake, he was researching early Fifties television. Although he won't admit it, I suspect he was first attracted to me because I reminded him of Gracie Allen. Along with a shared name, I bore an uncanny resemblance to the comedienne, including the eerie coincidence of having one blue eye and one green eye. The one difference being that although we were both born dark brunettes, the other Gracie had opted to go blonde.

Most importantly, though, like Gracie Allen, I tend to segue into slightly off-kilter rambling discourse that always makes sense to me but not necessarily to anyone else. The difference? Gracie Allen was acting; I'm not.

Now, after a quarter century of marriage, I'm still a brunette, although a slightly weightier one, still rambling to the tune of my own off-key and off-kilter symphony, and still Blake's Gracie. I'm not complaining.

His sarcasm aside, Blake Elliott is as sharp as aged Vermont cheddar. So if he said Sidney Mandelbaum was dead, I believed him. I crept a bit closer. Keeping Blake between Sidney and me, I peered over my husband's broad shoulders. The unfortunate Mr. Mandelbaum lay spread-eagle on the macadam. "Maybe we should have skipped from Client Twelve to Client Fourteen," I said. "Like the way floors are numbered in hotels and office buildings."

Blake stood and brushed his hands together. "Thirteen certainly wasn't Sidney's lucky number."

"Or ours. He said he was coming out for a smoke." I pointed to the unlit cigar and book of matches floating in the center of a blood puddle. "I've got a prospect waiting to meet him."

"Somehow I don't think he's up to it, sweetheart."

I swatted Blake's arm. "How can you joke at a time like this? Someone murdered one of our best paying clients."

Blake raised both eyebrows. "Me joking? What about thirteen?"

"I was serious." I pointed to Sidney. "This proves how unlucky the number thirteen is."

Sidney Mandelbaum was a serial *schmoozer*, and if you believed him, a serial *schtupper*. Like many single men his age, he'd entered his second randyhood thanks to the marvels of a little blue pill, which made him a desirable commodity among widows and divorcees of a certain age. And thank God for that because we needed the money. Sidney's murder was a definite financial setback for us.

The loss of Mandelbaum Moolah aside, Sidney wasn't just dead. I could fool myself into thinking his bashed in skull might be courtesy of a fall down the steep flight of concrete steps at the back of the Moose Lodge, but natural causes hadn't plunged a knife into his heart. "Omigod!"

Blake reached for me. "What?"

"What if the killer is still here?" I shuddered, quickly scanning the area for any movement, any lurking shadows.

"Go inside. Tell Mrs. What's-Her-Name—"

"Goldenberg."

"What?"

"Her name is Goldenberg. Ethel Goldenberg."

"Tell her he came down with a sudden case of—"

"Of what? Death?"

Blake waved his arms in the air as if he expected someone to slap a logical explanation into his hands. "Of food poisoning. The flu. Menstrual cramps. I don't know. Think of something. Before she comes looking for you." He pulled his cell phone from his coat pocket. "I'll call 911."

I stared at my normally levelheaded and always logical husband. "Menstrual cramps?"

Blake pointed to the door and mouthed, "Go."

I wasn't keen on leaving my husband alone with a dead body and a possibly loitering killer, but I could see the merit in keeping a heavy steel door between Mrs. Ethel Goldenberg and the man I had spent little more than five minutes convincing her to meet.

I ran up the steps as fast as my Kate Spade kitten heel mules would carry me, which admittedly wasn't all that fast. With a grunt and a yank, I opened the back door and went in search of the double-D cup retired bookkeeper who'd taken Client Number Thirteen's breath away—that is, while Client Number Thirteen still had breath.

Crap!

All I wanted to do was sit at my computer and write romance novels while Blake sat across the room and two-finger pecked away at *Pop Goes the Culture*, his epic tome on twentieth century culture and counter-culture and its influences on the media. Or vice versa. It was a real chicken-and-egg sort of thing as far as I was concerned, even if it was my husband's passion. Anyway, dead bodies weren't part of our empty nest blueprint.

I'd formulated a seven-step strategy for the next stage of our lives, going so far as to cross-stitch my plan and frame it over my desk because I believed in keeping both eyes on the prize. It's one of those management mantras they taught us at the mandatory team building retreats I used to attend back when I was gainfully employed as a fabric designer. Who would have thought you could outsource creativity to some Third World nation?

The sampler still hangs above my desk, but now it's more a taunt than a plan, an example of fate spitting in my eye.

PLAN FOR THE REST OF MY LIFE

1. Take early retirement.
2. Collect sizeable pension.
3. Pay off mortgage.
4. Write romance novels.
5. Sell romance novels.
6. Collect enormous royalty checks.
7. Live happily ever after with Pulitzer prize-winning husband.

Not that Blake had yet won a Pulitzer, or even been nominated for one, but I haven't given up hope. We need that prize money. Especially now.

But you know what they say about best-laid plans—they're bound to rear up and bite you in the tush. Six months later, when my unemployment compensation ran out and I still hadn't sold a book—since in most cases you actually have to write a book before you can sell one, and I was nowhere near finished—Blake informed me that I'd have to find a job.

"Or we can sell the house and move into an apartment over an auto repair shop in Newark," he said. "With double college tuitions, we can't afford your handbag bills, let alone much else on one income."

Just my luck I had to fall in love with a college professor instead of Warren Buffet or Donald Trump.

Since the smells of gasoline and car exhaust make me queasy and I have a deep-seated, must-own compulsion for every handbag du jour, I sat down at my computer and perused the postings at every online jobsite. I quickly struck out. No one wanted me.

I had just about resigned myself to spending the rest of my days working a minimum wage retail gig, where I'd at least get an employee discount, when I happened to come across an article about a phenomenon called Wing Women, an introduction service where women pose as longtime female friends to help guys meet other women.

That's when inspiration struck. Within two weeks Relatively Speaking was up and running, and I became a wing woman of sorts to the senior set.

I did mention I was creative, didn't I?

"So where's this handsome uncle of yours?" asked Mrs. Goldenberg when I found her piling a huge spoonful of ambrosia onto her already overflowing plate.

We had taken Sidney to the monthly five-dollar all-you-can-eat early bird social at the local Moose Lodge. Traditional twenty-something wing women escort their clients to trendy New York clubs. I take mine to various wildlife-with-antlers lodges, houses of worship, and senior citizen centers throughout New Jersey where elderly women usually outnumber the men by at least ten-to-one.

So why do the men need me? My job is twofold. I run interference between my clients and all the women they don't want zeroing in on them, and I offer assurance to the women. As desperate as they may be, they don't want to get hooked up with septuagenarian serial killers or gigolos.

Mrs. Goldenberg was one of three women "Uncle" Sidney had shown an interest in meeting that evening. But she was first on his list.

"The blonde with the casaba melons on her chest," said the none-too-subtle Sid, waving his unlit cigar in Ethel Goldenberg's direction. "Go. Do your thing, kid. She looks hot to trot, and I'm not getting any younger, you know."

He sent me off with a wink-wink and a pat to my tush that I was glad Blake didn't notice. My husband hadn't taken much of a liking to the boorish Sidney Mandelbaum.

Then again, neither had I, but at fifty dollars an hour with a three hour minimum, I could put up with the chauvinistic old coot for as long as his bank account held out. I had romance novels to write, and besides supplying the funds that allowed me to write them, Mr. Mandelbaum was juicy character research. Because Mr. Mandelbaum was quite a character.

Just so you don't get the wrong idea, I don't run a dating or escort service. All I do is mingle and chat with potential prospects, usually breaking the ice with a compliment—often the most difficult part of the evening, given most of these women wear polyester pantsuits and orthopedic shoes, carry vinyl (shudder!) handbags, and haven't updated their hairdos since Jackie Kennedy held court in the White House. After verifying their single status, I steer the conversation to my "uncle" or "father" or "my grandmother's second-cousin-once-removed on my mother's side." If the woman shows an interest, I introduce her to my client.

It's up to the client to do the rest. If the gods of second-time-around are smiling on him that night, he may go home with a few phone numbers and the promise of a future date. These are not people who meet in bars and hook up for one-night-stands, no matter how much the very recently departed Sidney Mandelbaum boasted about *schtupping live wires. Wink-wink.*

"I'm afraid Uncle Sid isn't feeling quite himself," I told Mrs. Goldenberg.

"Stomach trouble?" she asked. "My Arnold, may-he-rest-in-peace, had stomach trouble like you wouldn't believe." She rolled her eyes heavenward as she placed a liver-spotted hand on my arm. "What that poor man went through. And what I went through with him. The stories I could tell you—"

"It's not his stomach," I said, hoping to extricate myself from Mrs. Goldenberg before she launched into a graphic telling of *The Tales of Arnold's Intestines.*

"Oh, dear, not his heart, I hope." She removed her hand from my arm and placed it over her own heart.

I offered her a worried frown. "Afraid so. Stabbing pain." At least it wasn't a lie.

When I was four years old, my mother washed my mouth out with soap after I told her my sister had helped herself to the platter of brownies mom had baked for that night's PTA meeting. Too bad the evidence was spread all over my face and hands. To this day the very smell of Lifeboy makes me want to hurl.

Mrs. Goldenberg craned her turkey wattle neck, scanning the room behind me, no doubt, in search of a man clutching his chest. "Where is he? Have you called an ambulance? I should go to him."

As she set her overloaded, flimsy paper plate onto the crowded buffet table, a blob of marshmallow-topped orange Jell-O slid onto the roast beef platter. Mrs. Goldenberg made a *tsking* sound and brushed the ambrosia off with a wadded napkin. "Let's go," she said.

I reached for her arm. "I'm sure the ambulance is already here."

"But he shouldn't be with strangers at a time like this."

I started to remind her that *she* was a stranger, given I never had the opportunity to introduce her to the now dead senior Don Juan, but instead I said, "My husband is with him, and I think it's best we don't crowd the EMTs, don't you?"

Mrs. Goldenberg sighed. "Yes, I suppose you're right." She rifled through her purse until she found a pencil stub and a grocery receipt. "You give your uncle my number. Tell him to call me as soon as he's feeling up to it. I'll visit him in the hospital if he'd like. Every day. I'll make my chicken soup. My dear Arnold, may-he-rest-in-peace, said my chicken soup could cure the warts off a witch's nose."

I took the scrap of paper from her. "I'm sure Uncle Sidney will appreciate that," I said before hurrying toward the back exit.

By the time I slipped out the door, the parking lot was swarming with police. A tarp draped Sidney's body. Blake and two of the police officers stood off to the side next to a beat-up blue Oldsmobile.

Everyone turned at the sound of the metal door slamming shut behind me. Blake waved me over.

"This is my wife," he said to the officers. "Mr. Mandelbaum was her client." He gestured to first one, then the other. "Detectives Menendez and LaMotta."

Both nodded toward me. "Mind if we ask you some questions, ma'am?" asked Menendez, the older of the two, a woman about my age and height but easily fifty pounds heavier, all in muscle. She looked like she could bench press me without working up a sweat.

LaMotta, a head taller than Menendez, looked like he could bench press her. I was glad they were the good guys.

I rubbed my arms against the cool late summer breeze that had kicked up since I'd left Blake alone with the body. On the other side of the parking lot, stray trash blew up against the chain link fence. Ever the gentleman, Blake removed his navy summer blazer and slipped it over my shoulders. He left his arm draped around me.

"What would you like to know?" I asked Menendez.

The two of them peppered me with questions. How well had I known Sidney Mandelbaum? When had we met? Exactly what was our relationship? (That one caused some raised eyebrows and a bit of explanation.)

"Did you see anyone follow Mr. Mandelbaum outside?" asked LaMotta.

I gasped. "You can't possibly think one of the other seniors killed him! It had to be a random mugging, right?"

"We're just collecting information at this point, Mrs. Elliott. Please answer the question. Did you see anyone follow Mr. Mandelbaum outside?"

I shook my head. "No, but I really wasn't watching. I went to speak to Mrs. Goldenberg."

"And how long would you estimate Mr. Mandelbaum was gone before you went in search of him?" asked Menendez.

I thought for a moment. "Ten minutes? Maybe less."

"You're sure it wasn't longer?"

"No, Mrs. Goldenberg was quite interested in meeting Mr. Mandelbaum. When I couldn't find him anywhere in the lodge hall, I figured he was still outside, puffing away on his cigar. Blake and I came to get him."

Menendez and LaMotta stole a glance at each other. "Why both of you?" asked Menendez.

"Mr. Mandelbaum had wandering hands," Blake offered.

"And since those hands were helping feed us, I didn't want to risk losing a client by having to deck him," I added.

"So he was a dirty old man?" asked Menendez, raising an eyebrow in need of a good plucking.

I shrugged. "Sidney dabbled in borderline inappropriate

behavior. You know how old people are, not necessarily up on the latest political correctness."

In truth, Sidney's flirting fingers bothered Blake more than they did me. The textile industry, where I had worked my entire adult life, is rife with guys like Sidney Mandelbaum, and I learned early on how to deal with them without threatening sexual harassment lawsuits seventeen times a day. There's more than one way to skin the Sidney Mandelbaums of this world.

Blake's world was different. In academia, political correctness had turned into a zealous religion. Consequently, I have a higher tolerance for such nonsense than my husband. As long as Sidney kept himself to an occasional quick tush pat and didn't progress to groping, I was willing to put up with his coarseness in exchange for all the business he gave me. Life is a matter of trade-offs.

Menendez and LaMotta exchanged another glance. I wished they'd stop doing that. It reminded me too much of *The Look*. I shifted my weight from one foot to the other. My shouldn't-have-bought-them-but-they-were-on-sale-and-a-steal-so-who-could pass-up-such-a-bargain Kate Spade kitten heeled mules, the gold ones with the rhinestone trim, were pinching my bare, bordering on frostbitten, toes.

After a few more questions that seemed pretty inane and meaningless to me, Menendez and LaMotta finished their interrogation. Menendez handed me her card. "Call me if you remember anything else," she said.

Once they headed inside to question the assorted seniors, lodge members, and catering staff, I collapsed against my husband's chest. "Poor Mr. Mandelbaum," I said.

"Yeah, poor sleazy old Sid."

I sighed. "But he was a very well-paying old sleaze."

"I wonder who did him in," said Blake as we headed to our car.

I glanced up at my husband, surprised that I wasn't getting a now-do-you-see-why-I-didn't-want-you-getting-involved-in-this-cockamamie-idea-of-yours? lecture, but he was probably in shock over Sidney's murder. The lecture would come after the shock wore off.

Blake can be very overprotective. I think he sometimes wishes he'd taken a different career path, one that would have allowed his wife to stay in the kitchen baking cookies all day. But then he probably would have worried I'd burn down the house. Blake is an oxymoron—an unflappable worrywart.

"Not you, too? Come on, Blake. Sid was just in the wrong place at the wrong time, thanks to his need to light up. Knowing Sid, he tried to bargain the mugger down, and it cost him his life." Muggings were rare in the New Jersey suburbs, but they did happen from time to time and often to the elderly who are easy marks.

Blake clicked the button on his key fob to unlock our Camry. "I don't think so. And from what I gather, neither do the police."

I stopped and turned to face him as he held the car door open for me. Have I mentioned my husband is a gentleman? How many twenty-first century men open doors for women? I have to thank my mother-in-law for raising her son right. "Come on, Blake, you can't think someone deliberately set out to kill Sidney Mandelbaum."

Blake let go of the door handle and grasped my shoulders, holding me at arm's length. "After you went to speak to Mrs. What's-her-name—"

"Goldenberg."

Blake sighed before starting over, but to his credit he didn't give me *The Look*. "After you went to speak to Mrs. Goldenberg, the police found Sid's wallet in his pants pocket. Gracie, the guy had over six hundred dollars on him. This was no mugging. Unless he interrupted a drug deal—"

"In the Moose Lodge parking lot?"

"Exactly. Which means—"

"Someone intentionally killed Sidney Mandelbaum?" Every nerve in my body began to shudder and kept shuddering as I slid into the car. "Maybe someone interrupted the killer, and he didn't have time to find Sidney's wallet." But I found it hard to convince myself of that, let alone Blake. Wouldn't this fictional someone have run into the Moose Lodge for help?

I made three abortive attempts at fastening my seat belt before Blake took over and snapped the metal tongue into the slot for me. He might be the worrywart of the family, but his hands never shake.

Thinking sleazy old Mr. Mandelbaum had been the unfortunate victim of a mugging gone wrong was bad enough. Contemplating his death may have been at the hands of someone who specifically wanted him pushing up daisies was more than I could handle. I closed my eyes and took several deep breaths.

"You okay?" asked Blake after he settled himself behind the wheel.

"Not really." Aside from a case of uncontrollable shakes, my stomach felt like Mike Tyson had used it for a practice bag. I lowered my head into my lap and continued to inhale a few more deep breaths. "He was a harmless old man, for God's sake!"

Blake placed his hand on the back of my neck. "Do we really know that?"

I lifted my head and stared into my husband's deep teal eyes.

Blake's eyes were what first attracted me to him nearly thirty years ago. I was a lowly eighteen-year-old freshman; he was a twenty-four-year-old first year assistant professor assigned to teach English Comp to fifty art majors who wanted to be anywhere but in his classroom.

Luckily for us, there were no rules about student/faculty fraternization back then because a week later I was spending more time at his apartment than my dormitory room.

Teal always was my favorite color.

"Whatever. So maybe we didn't know all there was to know about Sidney." Everyone has secrets. I hardly expect my clients to divulge all of them to me when they fill out their application form. Still, Sidney didn't deserve to end up with a knife in his heart. "We have to find out who did this," I said, my newfound resolve overcoming my trembling limbs and sucker-punched stomach.

"*We?*" Blake raised both eyebrows and shot me *The Look*. "*We're* going to let the police handle this, Gracie."

"But—"

"No buts. I'm serious. This is totally out of your league. Don't go pulling an Anastasia Pollack on me. We're not characters in some book or TV show where there's always a happy ending on the last page or at the end of the hour. This is a real murder with real blood and a real killer."

"I know that."

"Good. Then think of me. Think of the twins. What would we do if anything happened to you?"

"The twins are nearly nineteen, off on their own most of the year, and you'd grab one of those Size Two coeds who are always throwing themselves at you."

Did I mention besides those deep teal eyes, Blake bears an

amazing resemblance to Hugh Jackman? Albeit, Hugh Jackman after that sexy shock of hair of his turns silver and his face develops deeper laugh lines around the corners of his eyes and mouth.

Forget all that feminist propaganda about God being a woman. If God were a woman, women would become distinguished as they aged, and men would just grow gray and wrinkled. Between that and women being the ones to suffer through the birthing process and menopause, God has to be a man. Any sensible woman would have figured that out a long time ago.

Blake's permanent laugh lines deepened into a scowl. "Have I ever given you any indication that I want one of those Size Two asses?"

I raised an eyebrow. Unlike Detective Menendez, I did take the time to pluck out any strays that threatened my perfect arch. "Not even in a fantasy or two?"

He leaned over and planted a kiss on my cheek. "From the moment I set eyes on your ass I wanted it starring in all my fantasies."

"Even though it's several sizes larger now?"

He settled back into his seat, started up the car, and shifted into reverse. "Even when you drive me crazy. Like now."

Of the two of us, Blake is the sensible one, the solid, staid, left-brained academician who analyses situations to death before making a decision. I'm the harebrained, right-brained partner who dives into the deep end head first, even though I can't swim. He's George Burns; I'm Gracie Allen—the poster couple for Opposites Attract.

And as much as I love my husband, I'd never been very good at taking orders. Anyway, I had a book to research. Thanks to Mr. Mandelbaum's untimely demise, my romantic comedy was quickly transforming into a romantic suspense. Now all I had to do was figure out who and why. If I happened to uncover Sidney Mandelbaum's killer along the way....

I smiled at Blake. "I'll be good," I said. And if I couldn't be good, I'd be careful. Careful not to let Blake know what I was up to.

TWO

After I came up with the idea for Relatively Speaking, I held off mentioning the new business to Blake until I had my first client. When my dear husband calmed down enough to keep from strangling me, he joined the company as a not-so-silent partner, but I knew it wasn't because he believed in my vision. He could care less about an introduction service for senior citizens. He only wanted to tag along to make sure I didn't cause a septuagenarian uprising or something. He probably also wanted to keep me away from any designer handbag stores.

"Good thing I have tenure," he'd said. "The last thing we need is this crazy scheme of yours blowing back on me. One of us out of work is bad enough."

Tenure or not, I didn't think the university could fire someone over a spouse's occupation, but I kept my mouth shut. Blake was the main breadwinner now. Not wanting to jeopardize his career, I'd previously agreed—reluctantly—to write my romances under a pen name because Blake had no idea how the governing board—

stuffy old academics that they were—might react to my sensual romances. For that reason, no one would ever know that Emma Carlyle, romance author, was actually Gracie Elliott, faculty wife.

Luckily, tenured senior professors also have fairly flexible hours because my work hours tend to be afternoons and early evenings. Most of my clients need several hours each morning to find their teeth and lube their creaky joints, not to mention deal with lower GI necessities. And they call it a night by eight o'clock. This schedule also gave me my mornings to write. I was making progress on my book and earning enough to keep us out of that apartment above the auto repair shop. At least one of us was happy with the situation.

Up until about an hour ago, I'd pooh-poohed Blake's concerns over what he had taken to calling "one of Gracie's more harebrained ideas." I, on the other hand, considered it one of my more brilliant, creative solutions, considering my growing waiting list of clients. Besides, how much trouble could I get into posing as some old geezer's daughter or niece or third-cousin-twice-removed?

Then Sidney had to go and get himself murdered. See what happens when you don't listen to your inner superstitions? I definitely should have skipped from Client Twelve to Client Fourteen.

After we returned home, I kicked off my mules and headed to the kitchen. Blake headed to the den to tackle a stack of student papers. At the beginning of the fall semester he assigns his first-year graduate students a twenty-five-hundred-word critical essay on how fifties television shaped the counter-culture of the sixties. Blake wrote his doctoral thesis on the subject (hence his knowledge of and fascination with George and Gracie as well as other sitcom families) and was familiar with every posted cyber-essay floating around the Internet. He'd even written a few of them.

Without fail, every one of his students hands in a downloaded essay. After receiving their F's, the students begin to realize they can't cheat their way to a master's degree—at least not in my husband's classes—and begin relying on their brains instead of Google.

"Well, here's a first," Blake said, coming up behind me as I prepared a salad to go with the salmon poaching on the stove. Both of us had passed on the culinary delights of the five-dollar all-you-can-eat early bird special at the Moose Lodge.

"What's that?" I asked.

With one hand he waved the paper in front of my face while his other hand reached around me to snag a cherry tomato. "Someone actually chose not to steal an essay off the Internet," he said, talking while chewing.

"Didn't your mother ever teach you not to talk with your mouth full?" I grabbed a towel and wiped a dribble of tomato juice from his chin.

Blake popped another cherry tomato into his mouth and spoke around it. "Guess I didn't pay attention to that lecture. Anyway, that's the good news."

"And the bad news?"

"The kid took the time to cobble together several posted essays."

"Maybe you should give him an F+. For effort and creativity.

"Her. Tiffany Robeling."

"Tiffany?" I snorted as I swatted the hand reaching for a third tomato. "In that case she was sucking up to you. Give her an F-, and leave some tomatoes for the salad."

Blake managed to secure the tomato anyway. After popping it

into his mouth, he planted a tomatoey kiss on my lips. "Trust me, the name doesn't fit the body. The kid has more piercing than St. Valentine. And those are only the ones visible to the public."

His comment triggered some painful images in my mind. "Ouch. I'm glad our kids never got into body mutilation."

"They call it art."

"Art?" I snorted again. "I went to art school. Trust me. Punching holes in your body wasn't one of the majors offered back then, and it still isn't."

"Self-expression, then. Different strokes, sweetheart. Don't start sounding like an old fogey."

I considered myself more free-spirited and creative than most people, but even I had my limits. And my body piercing stopped at a hole in each earlobe. "I wonder how they'll feel about all that self-expression when they're pushing fifty."

Blake laughed. "By then they'll have wised up and enhanced the coffers of many a plastic surgeon."

"Maybe I should have become a plastic surgeon."

"Right." Blake coupled *The Look* with *The Voice*.

"Could've happened. And we'd have a diplodocus-sized nest egg by now." Back when I chose to major in fabric design, who could have predicted I'd become obsolete at the not-ready-for-the-nursing-home age of forty-eight?

"At least I should have listened to my mother and become a teacher. Or a pharmacist. Maybe an accountant."

"You?" Blake raised an eyebrow. "Two words, Gracie: left brain."

"Oh yeah." Too bad I don't seem to have one. Never did. Math and science classes always scrambled my neurons. I'm a right-brained girl all the way.

Blake turned to leave but stopped when he noticed the folder on the counter. "What's this?"

"Sidney Mandelbaum's file."

Once again *The Look* settled across his face.

I turned my back and began slicing a zucchini. "I thought his application and the record of women he met through Relatively Speaking might shed some clues about who murdered him."

"Gracie..."

I sliced faster. "For the police, Blake. To help in their investigation." And mine. But I didn't mention that and kept my back turned to him so he couldn't read my face. "Go give Tiffany her F- and wash up for dinner."

~*~

The next morning while Blake delivered his standard lecture on research, integrity, and the Internet to a roomful of stunned Master's candidates, I hosted my writing critique group. Myra Fitzgerald, Natalie Davenport, and I had met when I joined Liberty States Fiction Writers. We bonded during a group critiquing session and had been meeting once or twice a week over coffee and manuscript pages ever since.

Like me, Myra and Natalie were both unpublished, but unlike me, both had finished at least one manuscript. Myra even had an agent shopping her work around. In my defense, both had been writing for several years before I ever sat my butt in a chair and placed my fingers on the keyboard to type the first sentence of my first novel. Obviously, I had some catching up to do. They didn't hold my lack of output against me, mainly because they valued my constructive criticism of their work. They also believed I had talent and encouraged me to keep writing.

"You'll never believe what happened yesterday," I said once I poured three cups of coffee and we settled around the dining room table.

"You finished your book?" asked Myra.

"You found an agent?" asked Natalie.

"I wish." I proceeded to tell them about the late Sidney Mandelbaum.

"Wow!" said Myra.

"Good thing Blake was with you," said Natalie.

"I know. Stumbling across a dead body is scary enough, but Sid wasn't just dead. He was murdered. Bashed in skull. Knife to the heart."

"Talk about rotten publicity," said Natalie. "The last thing you need is for some reporter to get hold of his connection to you."

"That's what I'm afraid of. Sidney's murder could wind up killing my business."

"How much do you know about the guy?" asked Myra.

"Only what he put down on his Relatively Speaking application."

"Do you do background checks of your clients?" asked Natalie.

The thought had never occurred to me. "No. Why?"

"Because as Gregory House was so fond of saying, 'Everyone lies.' For your own safety you should be checking out these guys before you start escorting them around, Gracie. What if some of them are up to no good? You could wind up either the victim of a crime or an accessory to a crime."

"Spoken like Natalie Davenport, master suspense author. These are sweet retired gentlemen I escort to senior citizens gatherings."

"I think Natalie is right," said Myra. "Look at all the creeps hanging out on Facebook and preying on young kids. We should at least Google this guy to make sure he was who he said he was."

"What's the point?" I asked. "He's dead. The victim of some random act of violence. Even though the killer didn't get Sid's wallet, it was still probably a hold-up gone bad."

"Then let's confirm your sweet old geezer was who he said he was," said Myra. "If we discover nothing odd, at least you'll have some peace of mind."

She made sense. We grabbed our coffee cups and traipsed upstairs to the office I shared with Blake. First I had to clear away the maze of index cards and sticky notes covering my desk. Before our trip to the Moose Lodge yesterday, I'd spent most of the day working out my hero's and heroine's internal and external goals, motivations, and conflicts.

After studying extensive how-to books, I'd learned there was more to creating a romance—comedic or otherwise—than just penning a steamy sex scene. Characters need to want something. They need a good reason for wanting that something. And they need something or someone to keep them from achieving that something. All this GMC, as it's known in the publishing world, is why I still hadn't finished my book. Besides stellar writing, I needed a hero and heroine with damn good GMC to make them stand out from all the other heroes and heroines being written by other romance author wannabes.

Once I'd transferred my jigsaw puzzle of notes to Blake's desk, I settled into my chair and typed Sidney's name into a Google search. Myra and Natalie hovered behind me, reading over my shoulders. A few clicks later we discovered Sidney had lied. Big time. And about everything.

"Uh-oh," said Myra as the three of us scanned the screen. According to the obituary that came up in my search, Sidney Mandelbaum had died of kidney failure two weeks prior to our first meeting.

"Crap!" I hate when I'm wrong and others are right. I grabbed the phone and dialed the Cedars of Lebanon Retirement

Community where my Sid had said he lived and where the other Sid had died. The receptionist confirmed they had had only one Sidney Mandelbaum in residence, the one who'd died over three months ago.

"So who was your Sid, and why did he lie to you?" asked Natalie.

Damned if I knew. I glanced at the wall-mounted clock. The last of Blake's students, dutifully chastised and assigned another essay, should have skulked out of his classroom by now. The phone still in my hand, I pushed the speed dial for his cell.

He answered with a question. "Staying out of trouble, Gracie?"

"Of course not."

Blake sighed. "I didn't think so. What's up?"

"When the police found Sid's wallet, did you notice any ID?"

"I saw his driver's license."

"Was it Sid's picture?"

"Of course. Why?"

I told him what the girls and I had discovered. "Our Sid stole that Sid's identity."

"And made himself a fake ID? The plot thickens. Did you call the cop who gave you her card? What was her name? Lopez? Gomez?"

"Menendez. My next call."

"Good. After you call her, go back on the Internet and verify the identities of all your other clients. No telling how many Sids you've got."

"You sound like Natalie. Sid's an anomaly."

"Natalie's right, and so am I."

"Come on, Blake. You think there's some sinister plot afoot involving senior citizens stealing the identities of dead men? And somehow they've gotten me mixed up in their nefarious scheme?"

I laughed. "You've been living with me too long. Your usually logical brain has veered off into creative right-brained territory. All my other clients are normal elderly gentlemen. The only thing wrong with them is that they're lonely and want to find some female companionship."

"You have empirical evidence to back up that claim, sweetheart?"

"I have something better."

"And what's that?"

"Gut instinct."

"Which served you so well with Sidney Mandelbaum."

Okay, so maybe my gut wasn't infallible, but it rarely failed me. "I'll admit I was blinded by Mandelbaum Moolah. All my other clients are on fixed incomes. Sid had an endless supply of money."

Most of my clients hire me for one or two events. They meet a few women and let nature take its course. Sid had booked a standing weekly sojourn into Little Old Lady Land.

Which begged two questions: Where did he get all those Franklins he spent so freely? And should I turn my romantic comedy into a romantic suspense or romantic mystery?

I posed the second question to Myra and Natalie.

"Maybe you should scrap your current work, start taking notes, and write a true crime book," suggested Myra.

"No, she's better off making stuff up," said Natalie. "For one thing, no one in law enforcement is going to share any details of an ongoing investigation with her."

"She's right," I said as I hunted around the office for Detective Menendez's business card. "I'm not a reporter. Anyway, it's more fun making things up."

"So play around with it for a few days," suggested Myra. "Bring what you come up with to Saturday's meeting."

Natalie shook her head. "I think you need to finish what you started, Gracie. You don't want to become one of those writers who jumps from one project to the next, never completing a manuscript. You'll never get published."

"You're right," I said as I continued to rifle through papers on my desk. "Besides, I can't leave Thea and Luke suspended in fiction purgatory. I brought them to life; I owe them a happily ever after."

"What are you looking for now?" asked Myra.

"The detective's card. I can't remember where I put it." I headed into the bedroom to check the purse I'd brought with me last night. The girls followed me.

"Are you sure you kept it?" asked Myra when a search through my Carla Mancini tan python-embossed leather hobo bag proved fruitless.

"I don't remember tossing it."

She and Natalie helped me search the rest of the bedroom. Natalie even got down on her hands and knees and checked under the bed. Going above and beyond friendship, Myra rooted through the wastebaskets in the bedroom and bathroom. Finding nothing, we headed downstairs and searched through the coupons, take-out menus, and repairmen business cards jammed into one of the kitchen drawers. *Nada.*

"What were you wearing last night?" asked Natalie.

"Nothing with pockets but—" I raced back upstairs, Myra and Natalie close behind. Opening Blake's closet, I searched for the blazer he'd draped over my shoulders last night. Sure enough, when I stuck my hand in the jacket's pockets, I found Detective Menendez's card in one of them.

By this point we'd wasted over an hour and a half without reading a single page of anyone's manuscript. Myra announced she had to leave for a doctor's appointment, and Natalie had a client meeting in half an hour. They both headed out while I placed my call to Detective Loretta Menendez.

~*~

When the doorbell rang twenty minutes later, I expected to find Detective Menendez standing on my front porch. Instead, I opened the door to find two men in black. Mirrored sunglasses. Conservative suits. White shirts. Red and black striped tie on one, red and navy striped tie on the other. Short cropped hair. Grim expressions.

The black stripe spoke first. "Mrs. Elliott?"

"Yes."

He flipped open a leather wallet he held in his hand and flashed a badge and ID. "I'm agent Remick," he said, snapping the case closed. "This is agent Craft." Navy stripe flipped open his leather case. Another badge and ID.

My gaze shifted back and forth between them. "FBI?"

"That's right, ma'am," said Craft. "We'd like to ask you a few questions about Sidney Mandelbaum."

"I'm expecting Detective Menendez."

The two feds shot a quick glance at each other. "Menendez?" asked Remick.

"She's off the case," said Craft.

"Why?"

"May we come in, ma'am?"

Did I have any choice? What were the laws regarding FBI showing up at your door? If I refused, would I be arrested under the Patriot Act? Maybe Sid was involved in some terrorist plot and using me as his cover.

Laugh all you want, but who would suspect a Jewish septuagenarian terrorist operating in Union County, New Jersey?

What a perfect cover. Maybe Sid passed along secret government information to little old lady spies during our weekly trips to those senior socials.

Which made me an accessory to a crime. Not to mention a traitor. And if I remembered correctly from U.S. History back in high school, the penalty for that was death.

Crap! All I wanted to do was write romance novels. All of a sudden I'm seeing myself blindfolded in front of a firing squad. Blake was not going to be happy.

Hoping I'd gain brownie points and a presidential pardon by cooperating, I opened the door wider, ushered the two men inside, and led them to the living room. "Excuse the mess," I said, gathering up several overstuffed white plastic Target bags I'd dumped on the sofa the previous day in my rush to get to the bathroom.

After birthing twins and the onset of menopause, my bladder was showing signs of age. Apparently, so was my memory because I'd totally forgotten about the bags laden with Tide, Bounty, Charmin, Pepto-Bismol, and a package of sixty-watt light bulbs. Good thing I'd been to Target and not ShopRite. Otherwise I might have congealed, melted ice cream all over my Ethan Allen sofa.

I dumped the bags on the floor next to the piano. "Have a seat, gentlemen."

They remained standing, their massive presence seeming to take up half my living room. "We understand you have some information you were going to turn over to Detective Menendez," said Remick.

"Some files?" added Craft, as if he thought he needed to nudge my brain.

"Sure. I'll get them for you." I grabbed the shopping bags and headed into the kitchen. Dropping the sacks on the counter, I jogged up the back stairs to the office and grabbed Sid's file.

When I turned around to head back downstairs, I slammed smack into Remick's chest. "Jeez, you...you scared the c...crap out of me!" I sucked in the air he'd knocked from my lungs.

The man must be part cat. I never heard him climb the stairs or walk down the hall. And we have hardwood floors. No plush carpet to cushion the sounds of hundred-year-old wood creaking under the weight of a two-hundred pound man. No wonder they call them spooks. Or is that the CIA?

Remick didn't bother to apologize, only offered me an icy stare as he took the folder from my hand. "Is this all?" he asked.

I nodded. "Sid's application and a list of the women he met through Relatively Speaking. That's all I have in the way of paperwork on him. So who was he, really?"

Remick opened the file. Somehow he managed to peruse the contents while keeping one eye on me. "What do you mean?"

I told him about my Google search. "He wasn't Sidney Mandelbaum, was he? And why is the FBI investigating his murder? Was Sid a terrorist?"

Remick raised an eyebrow. His mouth quirked into what I supposed came as close to a smile as he ever got, even if it looked more like a sneer. He snorted. "You've got some imagination, lady. Maybe you should write a book."

Right. Why did I get the feeling Remick knew more about me than I knew about him? Although I was thinking of turning my romantic comedy into a romantic suspense or romantic mystery, I hadn't yet begun to do any online research that might send up red flags on Carnivore or Echelon, but I had recently joined an online mystery/suspense writing loop that discussed all sorts of criminal activities. Did the FBI routinely lurk on Yahoo groups?

At least Remick had allayed my fears of Sid being a terrorist. Figuring I no longer had to worry about a treason charge, I removed the imaginary blindfold from my eyes and scattered the firing squad from my brain. So why else would the FBI be involved in Sid's murder? "Was Sid in Witness Protection?" I asked.

Remick's mouth flattened into a straight, tight line. His eyes narrowed. "I'm not at liberty to discuss the case," he said.

Bingo! Maybe I should forget about introducing seniors and turn Relatively Speaking into a detective agency. I fought to suppress a smile but failed miserably. I'd make a lousy actress. Or FBI agent.

Remick glared at me. "We'll be on our way now."

He waited for me to leave the room, then followed me down the stairs and back into the living room where we found Craft standing in front of the fireplace. He'd removed one of the photo albums from the bookcase and was flipping through the pages. "Good looking family," he said, placing the album back on the shelf.

"Thank you." I walked them to the door and watched as they climbed into a black SUV parked at the curb and drove off.

Five minutes later the doorbell rang again. "Forget to ask me something?" I asked as I opened the door.

"Excuse me?"

"Detective Menendez! I didn't expect you."

Her in-need-of-a-good-plucking brows bunched together. "You called me, Mrs. Elliott. Remember?"

"But the FBI said you were taken off the case."

"FBI?"

"Agents Remick and Craft. They came for Sid's file. You missed them by minutes."

Menendez stared at me as if I were speaking in Tongues. "Mrs.

Elliott, my husband is a field agent with the FBI. I can assure you there are no agents named Remick and Craft operating in this state. And I was definitely *not* taken off the Mandelbaum case."

THREE

I stared at Menendez and felt her words sinking to the pit of my stomach—like my mother-in-law's lard-laden pie crusts. "But I saw their badges and ID," I said.

She made a noise that sounded halfway between a grunt and a snort. "Bogus. Bought over the Internet, no doubt. It's a huge problem." She shook her head. "I don't suppose you made a copy of that file before giving it to them?"

Contrary to what she thought of me, I wasn't an idiot. Not only did I have a paper copy, I had the original records on my computer and a backup on a jump drive in a waterproof and fireproof lock box. I had an extreme fear of both natural disasters and IRS audits. And chances were, if we were struck by the former, that would be the year our name randomly popped up on the IRS roulette wheel.

Menendez followed me upstairs. "What did these guys look like?"

"Big." I turned to her after we'd entered the office. She held a small pad in one hand, a pencil poised over it. "Like weight lifters or football players on steroids."

Menendez looked up from her notepad and stared at me.

"All muscles. No necks."

"No necks?"

"Haven't you ever noticed you can tell whether an athlete is on steroids by his lack of neck?"

"Can't say that I have." She jotted something on her pad. "Anything else?"

"You don't believe me, do you?"

"About the FBI agents?"

"About the steroids."

She sighed. "I don't think there's any scientific proof to back up your theory."

"If there were proof, it wouldn't be a theory; it would be fact."

Her steely expression told me she wasn't buying it. "What else can you tell me about these men?"

"Check out the necks. You'll see I'm right."

"Sure." Menendez sighed again.

She had no intention of checking out my theory. I could tell she was only humoring me. That's the problem with most people. They're too left-brained, afraid to think outside the box.

"Can we get back to what you remember, Mrs. Elliott? You didn't by any chance catch the license plate of the car they drove off in, did you?"

"Why would I think to do that when I believed they were FBI agents?"

"Right." She expelled a third sigh.

"I did recognize the make and model." Not that I'm a car nut but Blake's cousin Anthony owns a Mercedes dealership, and he's always trying to get us to trade up. Every time we see him at a family function he just happens to have a new brochure for us. And everyone else. Like Blake and I could afford a Mercedes, with our two kids in college and being down to one steady paycheck.

"Which was?" asked Menendez.

"A Mercedes SUV. Black with tinted windows."

She scribbled in her notebook. "Anything else you remember?"

While I offered what I remembered of the phony agents' physical traits and attire—which didn't seem to impress Detective Menendez, judging from her lack of jotting—I printed out a second set of Not-Sid's records. "He wasn't Sidney Mandelbaum, by the way," I said, handing her the sheets of paper. "But I'm guessing you already figured that out."

Menendez went all stony-faced on me. "How do you know that?"

I motioned to the computer. "The marvels of Google. I only wish I'd checked him out before I accepted him as a client." I should have known all that Mandelbaum Moolah was too good to be true, especially with the financial U-turn my life had taken over the past year. "So who was he? And why was he pretending to be someone he wasn't?"

Menendez remained stony-faced. Her lips barely moved as she spoke. "I'm not at liberty to discuss an ongoing investigation. Thank you for the files, Mrs. Elliott." With that she turned on her low, sensible heels and headed for the stairs.

"That's it?" I asked, trotting down the steps behind her.

She stopped in the foyer and turned to face me. "What do you mean?"

"*What do I mean?* Jeez, it doesn't take an Olivia Benson to see there's something odd going on here, Detective. I have some goons posing as FBI agents show up at my door, asking for stuff only you, me and my husband should know about, and all I get is a 'thank you for the files, Mrs. Elliott'? I'm a little creeped out here, and I'd like to know what you guys plan to do about it. Is my phone tapped?"

"Not by us."

"But maybe by the goon squad?" I planted my hands on my hips and went on the offensive. "Who are those guys? What do they have to do with Sid's murder? Why did they want my files on him? If they're not the good guys, I have a right to know what's going on here. Was Sid—or whoever he was—involved in something illegal?"

She stared at me for nearly a full minute. Or at least it felt that long. In reality, maybe only a few seconds elapsed before she waved toward the living room and heaved yet another huge sigh. "Sit down, Mrs. Elliott. I could wind up with my butt in a sling for this, but I suppose I can answer a few questions."

Crap! I didn't like the sound of that. My legs wobbled as I made my way over to the living room, and it wasn't from wearing too-high Manolos or Jimmy Choos. I was barefoot due to the fact that more often than not, my feet rebelled against my fashionista sensibilities. Along with designer handbags, I loved designer shoes; they hated my slightly chubby feet. A fact I was always reminded of too late—after I'd bought a pair and worn them for a few hours. I slumped onto the sofa and held my breath, waiting for Detective Menendez to drop a bombshell or three.

She perched on the edge of the oversized tufted leather ottoman that served as our coffee table. "We don't know who the victim was," she said, letting loose the first bombshell. "We're working on it."

This filled me with all sorts of confidence about the local constabulary, especially considering Remick and Craft obviously knew Sid's real identity. "Did you run his prints?" I asked, applying some of my *NYPD*, *CSI*, and *Law & Order* knowledge.

Menendez scowled. "The deceased had no prints."

"Everyone has fingerprints. Even I know that much."

"True, but some people go to great lengths to eradicate them. In the victim's case, the evidence points to the use of acid."

Acid? Bombshell Number Two. Why hadn't I noticed Not-Sid's lack of fingertip whorls? I certainly had a more than passing association with the man's hands.

"So whoever he was," Menendez continued, "he went to drastic lengths to conceal his identity. And that's all I can tell you."

Which wasn't much. "Am I in any danger?"

She tapped the papers in her hand as she stood. "I doubt it. Whoever Remick and Craft are, they got what they wanted. I don't think you'll hear from them again."

I rose. "But how did they know about me?"

"They could have been tailing the victim for some time." She headed for the front door.

"So you think Remick and Craft killed Not-Sid?"

Menendez stopped. Her hand poised on the doorknob, she turned to face me. "That's one possibility."

Great! Not only had I let possible killers into my home, I now had to warn Blake about my morning visitors, something that until now I'd thought I might be able to avoid.

As I headed back upstairs after Menendez left, I glanced into the living room. Something half hidden beneath the back rung of the mission oak rocker caught my eye.

I headed back downstairs, picked up the snapshot, and pulled the photo album it had fallen from off the shelf. When I flipped opened the album to return the photo, Bombshell Number Three hit. Several pictures of Blake, me, and our twins were missing.

Blake was going to have a cow, and I wouldn't blame him. What had I gotten us into?

I didn't have to wait long for Blake's reaction. He arrived home about half an hour later.

"Want a latte?" he asked after dropping his briefcase on his desk and planting a kiss on my lips.

I had spent the last thirty minutes staring at Not-Sid's file, trying to figure out who the man was and why he wanted to meet so many women. What would a man who went to such lengths to disguise his identity want with me and Relatively Speaking? No matter how long I studied the pages, I came up blank. Some huge chunk of the puzzle was missing, a huge chunk that somehow involved Remick and Craft. And not in a good way.

"Sure," I said and followed Blake downstairs. "You might want to spike those with something," I suggested as he headed for the espresso machine we kept on the kitchen island.

He gave me *The Look.*

I opened a cabinet and pulled out a bottle of Hiram Walker. "I had a few visitors today," I said, passing Blake the bottle.

"Am I going to want this straight up?" he asked.

"What I have to tell you or the whiskey?"

"Both."

I cringed. "Maybe?"

Blake set the bottle on the counter and crossed his arms over his chest. "Let's have it, Gracie."

I took a deep breath and blurted out everything that had happened since he left that morning. Halfway through my tale, he sank onto one of the bar stools at the island, buried his head in his hands, and began cursing under his breath.

And I hadn't even gotten to Bombshell Number Three yet. "You didn't by any chance take any photos out of one of our albums, did you?"

Blake raised his head and stared at me. "That's a pretty odd non sequitur, even for you."

I bit my lower lip. "Not really."

"What aren't you telling me?"

"Craft stole half a dozen snapshots of us."

Up until that moment I hadn't realized my husband could swear in seven different languages. I knew he was fluent in French, Italian, and Spanish, and the man could bluff his way around a German knockwurst or opera. But who would have guessed his repertoire of foreign profanity included what sounded like Hungarian and Farsi? Granted, I didn't know Hungarian from Bulgarian and Farsi from Afghani, but some of those words certainly sounded Slavic and others were definitely Mideast in flavor. At any rate, after all these years, my husband still surprises me.

"Finished?" I asked after he'd run through his entire repertoire of four-letter words three times.

He reached for the Hiram Walker and unscrewed the cap. "Not quite." After taking a swig from the bottle, he passed it to me and reached for my hand. "Sorry for the outburst, Gracie, but you've scared the shit out of me."

"I'm not doing so well myself," I said. Then I took a swig. "I'm frightened, Blake. And the police don't seem to be too concerned about our safety. I called Menendez as soon as I discovered the missing photos. She said she'd make sure someone patrolled the house, but she thinks Craft deliberately left the photo where I'd find it, so I'd notice the missing pictures. She thinks they just want to scare me, that they got what they came for."

"I get the feeling you don't agree with her?"

"Hell, no! They have no clues, no leads, other than my files. So how can she be so sure about Craft's reason for stealing the photos?"

"There's another possibility," he said. "The files may have nothing to do with the murder."

"Then why would Remick and Craft go to such lengths to get their hands on them?"

"To misdirect the police? Create false clues?"

I mulled over that for a minute. "Or maybe Remick and Craft are after something Not-Sid had and think he may have hidden it with one of the women he met through Relatively Speaking."

"Or with us. Maybe this would be a good time for you to go visit your sister in Florida."

"What? And leave you here alone? Absolutely not! Besides, what guarantee do we have that I won't be followed to Florida?"

"So what do you suggest?"

I tossed Blake my most endearing smile. "You and I solve Not-Sid's murder."

He let loose with another string of foreign obscenities.

"Was that Russian, Ukrainian, or Serbian? And that last one...Greek? I swear, you never cease to amaze me."

He groaned. "Gracie, what the hell do we know about solving murders?"

"Apparently about as much as the police in this county. And I'm not willing to sit back and wait for them to blunder their way to a solution, are you?"

He mulled over my words for a moment. "No. Not when my wife's safety is at stake. So what did you have in mind?"

"We start with MOM."

Blake stared at me as though I'd suggested we take a swim in a tank full of killer sharks. "What the hell does your mother have to do with this? And why on earth would you want to get her involved?"

"Nothing. And I don't."

"But you just said—"

"MOM. It's an acronym for motive, opportunity, and method. Mystery writers use it to plot novels."

Blake shook his head. "Mystery writers make up murders and suspects. They don't solve real crimes. You can't apply the same logic."

I shrugged. "Why not? We already know two pieces of the puzzle: We know what the murder weapon was, and the killer found his opportunity when Not-Sid stepped outside for a cigar. All we need to do is figure out the motive, and we'll find the killer."

Blake raised an eyebrow, accompanied by *The Look* and *The Voice*. "Oh, is that all? Well, what are we waiting for? We should have this case wrapped up by dinner."

"Sarcasm doesn't suit you, darling."

"And deductive reasoning isn't one of your strong suits, sweetheart. There are more holes in your logic than in a brick of Swiss."

I smiled at him. "That's why I have you to help me. I'll do the creative thinking; you plug up the holes with that left-brained logic of yours. Between us, we'll make a terrific team. And catch a killer."

Blake reached for the whiskey bottle. Before he took another swig, he muttered something that sounded like a mix of Japanese and Portuguese

FOUR

I grabbed Hiram out of Blake's hand and placed him back on the shelf. "Lattes," I said pointing to the espresso machine.

My husband wasn't prone to binge drinking. He wasn't even prone to social drinking other than an occasional glass of wine at a restaurant or faculty cocktail party. The last time we'd engaged in a threesome with Hiram was the day I learned my job had packed up and moved to China, leaving me with a zero balance in my 401K and no prospect of a pension. But I wasn't taking any chances. We both needed sober wits about us if we were going to solve Not-Sid's murder.

After Blake added steamed milk to the espresso, I grabbed the two glass mugs and headed for the stairs. "Where are you going?" he asked.

"Upstairs to start sleuthing."

He followed after me. "I'll admit I'm new to the Sherlock Holmes thing, Gracie, but I'm pretty sure Sid's killer isn't hiding under one of our beds."

I shoved his latte at him and settled into my desk chair. "Very funny, Dr. Watson, but since you brought up Sherlock Holmes—"

I reached for one of my how-to-write-a-mystery books. Even though I knew I was a romance writer at heart—due to a desperate need for every story to have a happily-ever-after—when I first began researching the ins and outs and ups and downs of romance writing, I had also familiarized myself with the whys and wherefores of other genres. Given that I'd now decided to transform my romantic comedy into a romantic suspense or mystery, my research was paying off.

After leafing through the first few pages, I shoved the book into Blake's free hand and pointed to a line of text. "Read what the master says."

Blake read out loud. "'When you have eliminated the impossible, whatever remains, however improbable, must be the truth.'" He lifted his gaze from the page and directed his attention back to me. "Setting aside the fact that your *master* is a fictional character, your point?"

"Don't you see? One of the women Not-Sid met through Relatively Speaking probably holds the key to his murder. All we have to do is eliminate all the ones who don't, and we'll have our answer."

Blake took a sip of his latte. "Or not."

I grabbed the book out of his hand and snapped it closed. "Don't be so negative."

"I'm not being negative. I'm being logical. Isn't that my role in your sleuthing scheme? Who's to say any of the women know anything? Sid was a randy old goat living a double life. For all we know, he's got a wife in Piscataway and a mistress in Parsippany.

Maybe he's a retired printer and destroyed his fingertips from decades of pulling zinc plates out of etching baths."

I stared at my own fingers. Four years of printmaking classes in college hadn't affected my whorls, but maybe after a lifetime of working with corrosive chemicals without protective hand coverings, some professional printers had little left of their fingerprints. I had no idea if that was possible. I also had no clue about Not-Sid's preretirement occupation. He'd never mentioned anything about his past.

"And don't you think the police are already questioning the women he met through you?" continued Blake. "If there's anything to find out, they'll find it."

Damn him and his logic. The world didn't operate on logic; it operated on random whim, passion, and chaos. But Blake had started his career as a math major before he'd realized his true academic calling. Unfortunately, too many logarithms, cosines, and hypotenuses still floated around in his brain.

I shook my head. "I'll bet Menendez intimidates those women. She's not exactly all warm and fuzzy, you know? And an intimidated person is one who either clams up or conveniently forgets things."

"Says who?"

"I read it in one of my research books."

"I'm guessing that wouldn't be a police procedural manual on interviewing witnesses."

"I think it was the book on character traits." I took a step toward the bookcase that housed all my research books. "Want me to find it for you?"

"That's okay. I'll take your word for it." He waved his half-empty mug in my direction. "Lead on, Holmes. I'm at your service.

Where would you like to begin?"

I grabbed the list of women Not-Sid had dated and gave it a quick glance. Upon earlier perusal, nothing had jumped out at me, but I'd only spent a short amount of time with each of the women before introducing them to Not-Sid. I had no idea how much time they'd spent with him afterwards. If any. Some of them may have had second thoughts and declined what I imagined, knowing Sid, was his invitation for bagels and lox au natural.

Then again, most of these women had struck me as the type who'd suggest the au natural themselves. One thing I'd learned in the short time I'd operated Relatively Speaking—these were not my grandmother's septuagenarians. Today's senior women were either living active sex lives or hoping to. And not shy to speak about it. Made me shudder to think how my mother was spending her retirement down in Del Rey Beach, Florida. *Yikes! Don't go there, Gracie.*

I glanced up at Blake. "Promise me I can die first."

"What?"

"I'll even give you permission to take up with one of your sexy students afterwards. I don't care."

Blake pulled me toward him and kissed the tip of my nose. "Do I want to know what precipitated this out-of-the-blue concern?"

"I don't want to wind up desperate enough to get the hots for someone like Sid." I swatted his chest with my palm. "Now promise me."

Blake sighed. "I promise. Happy?"

"Okay." I wriggled out of his arms and turned my attention back to the list of Not-Sid's dates. "Let's start with Sylvia Schuster. She was Not-Sid's last hook-up this past Tuesday evening."

"Hook-up? You do know what that means nowadays, don't

you?"

Did I?

"Friends with benefits hook-up."

Okay, so I'm not the quickest bunny in the warren. It took a minute for Blake's words to process. "That's not what I meant!" Ugh! Septuagenarian sex. The thought grossed me out. And made me wonder again just what my sweet widowed mother was doing down in Del Rey Beach.

But maybe Sylvia and Sid did wind up doing the horizontal jitterbug Tuesday night, thanks to me and my grand idea for a business.

~*~

Sylvia Schuster resided at Larchmont Gardens, an upscale adult community tucked away on the edge of the Watchung Reservation in Union County. No Indians. The reservation is a park and wildlife preserve in the Watchung Mountains, but Indians probably roamed the trails at one time. If I'd paid more attention back in elementary school instead of doodling in the margins of my loose-leaf notebooks, I'd probably know for sure.

Now the Reservation is the hub of a wheel whose spokes branch off into some of the priciest communities in the state, pricey enough that *Wheel of Fortune* often gives away shopping spree vacations at the local Mall at Short Hills, a mall I once loved but where I can no longer afford to shop, thanks to my current pathetic financial situation. *Au revoir* Neiman Marcus, Saks, Bloomie's, and Nordstrom. Hello (ugh!) WalMart, KMart, and Dollar Store.

We found Sylvia Schuster engrossed in a Mah Jongg game in the solarium. A diminutive dumpling of a woman with a steel gray, slightly off-center beehive, she wore a lavender polyester pantsuit that had what looked like a smear of dried grape jelly in the vicinity of her left breast. At least the stain color-coordinated with her outfit.

I waved from the doorway to catch her attention. "Hi, Mrs. Schuster. Remember me?"

She tossed a tile into the center of the card table where she sat with three other women. "One bam. I remember you. Have a seat," she said without looking up from her rack of tiles.

"South," said another woman, also tossing a tile into the pile.

I glanced around the room. All the other chairs were occupied, so Blake and I stood off to the side and watched as the women continued their ten-finger tap dance with the tiles. "You have any idea how this game works?" I whispered.

"Chinese gin rummy of sorts. Except they use tiles instead of cards."

I tried to follow along but quickly gave up. When it came to card games, I stuck with Fish and Old Maid. "Greek to me," I said.

Blake gave me *The Look*, but I detected a hint of a crinkle around his eyes and the corners of his mouth.

We watched as the four women took turns, reaching for and discarding tiles in a fashion as rapid-fire as a Mafioso with an Uzi. Trying to keep up with the quick tempo action made me dizzy. The women spoke in some kind of code as they tossed the tiles.

"Two crack."

"East."

"Red."

"Four bam."

I soon gave up trying to figure out what they were doing and turned my attention to the plant-filled solarium. A dozen wooden card tables were scattered about the room. Four women sat at each, all tossing bams and cracks and assorted colors and compass directions. Several motorized scooters were parked around the perimeter of the room. Metal walkers stood next to many of the women's chairs. But you'd never know these ladies had trouble getting around from the way their arthritic hands grabbed and tossed those tiles. If the Olympics held a hot potato tournament, I had no doubt every woman in that room would qualify.

Finally, Sylvia yelled, "Mahjongg!" A Cheshire grin plastered from ear to ear, she reached across the table and made a beckoning motion with the fingers and outstretched palms of both her hands. "Come to mama, my pretty green babies."

"Fleeced again," grumbled one of the women.

"She cheats," said another, a generously proportioned woman with a double chin, jet black hair, and rhinestone embellished cat's eye glasses.

Sylvia's grin turned wicked. "Prove it, Blanche."

"I'm working on it."

The women took their time methodically counting out fives, tens, and twenties. "Serious stakes," said Blake under his breath.

From my slightly obstructed vantage point, I estimated Sylvia pulled in three hundred dollars. Damn. I had to put up with the likes of Sidney Mandelbaum for six hours in order to make three Franklins. And now that Sid was gone, I wasn't going to see that kind of money nearly as fast as I did when he was alive and eager to schmooze the elderly ladies of northern and central New Jersey.

"Maybe I should take up Mahjongg," I said.

Blake cleared his throat in an attempt to squelch a chortle. He wasn't successful. "You might have better luck finding a competitive Candyland league," he suggested.

Sometimes it annoys the hell out of me that my husband

knows me so well. This was one of those times.

One by one the women grudgingly handed neatly folded bundles of bills to Sylvia. After recounting each wad, she stuffed the money inside the pink and lavender floral blouse that peeked out from beneath her polyester suit jacket. "Same time next week, ladies?"

"What? You've already stolen what's left of my Social Security check for this month," said Blanche. With a grunt, she pushed away from the table and wobbled over to a burgundy scooter a few feet from where Blake and I stood. I glanced down at her legs. She wore a pair of hot pink Capri pants over sagging support hose. And I swear those were Manolos on her feet. I remembered drooling over a similar pair of strappy silver sandals with Swarovski crystals the last time I dared to window shop along Fifth Avenue.

"Like Blanche needs her Social," stage whispered the woman seated to Sylvia's left. She grabbed her walker and hauled her more than ample girth to her feet.

"Where are you all going? What about lunch?" asked Sylvia.

The woman turned back and patted Sylvia's hand. "We ate lunch an hour ago, dear."

Sylvia's brows knit together. "We did? Are you sure, Pearl?"

"Yes. You had a chef's salad, a cup of tomato bisque, and a jelly donut."

That explained the purple stain.

"Did I enjoy it?"

Blanche made a snorting sound deep in her throat as she hoisted herself onto her scooter. "Talk about selective memory," she muttered. "The woman can't remember eating lunch an hour ago, but she remembers every single Mahjongg tile anyone plays."

After scowling at Sylvia, Blanche started up her scooter and raced toward the door, nearly running over Blake's foot as she sped across the low pile industrial carpet.

Pearl and the third woman exchanged conspiratorial looks with Sylvia before they shuffled away behind their walkers. I swore I heard them titter as they left the solarium.

Finally, Sylvia turned her attention to us. "Poor Blanche. All the money in the world couldn't buy her a sense of humor. Bitter old pill of a woman." She chortled. "I just love yanking her chain. And parting her from some of that ill-gotten slum money of hers. Makes my day, as that sexy Clint Eastwood says."

My jaw dropped involuntarily. "So that bit about not remembering lunch—?"

"All an act." Sylvia patted her beehive like a preening bird. "I used to be an actress, you know. Back in the late fifties and early sixties."

I shook my head. Our one previous conversation had lasted all of ten minutes and hadn't included Sylvia's professional résumé from over half a century ago. My job was to find out if the women my clients were interested in meeting were single and interested in meeting them. Period.

"In early television," she added.

"Really?" Blake suddenly grew quite interested in Sylvia Schuster but not for the reason behind our visit.

Sylvia sat up a bit straighter and thrust her knockers in his direction. Age never mattered. Young or old, women always zeroed in on my man. "I was the original Karpet King housewife," she said with a bat-bat, flutter-flutter of her eyelashes.

I forced myself to suppress a giggle as I watched my husband's hopes—and his expression—plummet.

"And I never even had to audition," Sylvia continued. "My uncle knew I was perfect for the role. Said I had natural talent."

"Your uncle?" I asked.

"Melvin Kronstein. He started the Karpet King chain. But then I met Edgar, and he didn't think it would be proper for a married woman to lounge around seductively on broadloom. Men had very old-fashioned ideas back then." She sighed, her voice growing wistful. "If not for Edgar, who knows where my career would have taken me? My Lady Macbeth received rave reviews in nineteen-fifty-eight."

"On Broadway?" I asked.

"In Newark. Weequahic High School. But that's all in the past. I married Edgar. Then I married Stanley. Then I married Irving. Three husbands, five children. Who had time for anything else?"

The way Sylvia rambled and jumped headlong from one subject to another sounded eerily familiar. She reminded me of someone. When I caught the expression on Blake's face, I knew. Blake was giving Sylvia *The Look*. My God! Sylvia reminded me of me!

This was not good. Poor Blake! Is that what he had to look forward to twenty-five or thirty years from now? I made a mental note to work on curbing my excessive right-brain-itis. It was the least I could do for my husband. I refused to doom the poor man to living with the likes of Sylvia in his golden years.

The scatterbrain in question patted the chair beside her. "Sit. Tell me what sort of trouble that conniving, phony uncle of yours got himself into."

My jaw dropped. "You know he wasn't my uncle?"

Sylvia's eyes twinkled. "I wasn't born yesterday, sweetie. You think I don't keep up? You're a wing woman, right? That lovely

Katic Couric did a piece on them a few months ago. Pegged you for one the moment you started chatting me up during the reception for that local politician. You have *chutzpah*; I'll give you that much. When I was your age..." She shrugged the thought away. "No matter. Like I said, things were different back then."

I glanced at Blake. Having lost interest in Sylvia, he had strolled over to the corner of the room and was pretending to ignore me, his attention engrossed instead on an oddly shaped, sepia colored water stain that spread across several ceiling tiles.

Like my handyman-challenged husband cared a flying fig about water stains! Or ceiling tiles. I could tell he'd heard every word and was forcing himself to keep from laughing. He'd warned me no one would believe I was my client's daughter. Or niece. Or third-cousin-twice-removed.

I didn't care. Authors create successful fiction by getting their readers to suspend disbelief. Especially in romance fiction. Considering the rate of divorce in this country, the idea of happily-ever-after is as humongous a suspension of disbelief as there is. I merely applied the same theory to my business model. The setup was just the feather that initially tickled the interest of the women I approached on behalf of my clients. Whether they believed my relationship to the men who hired me or not, I was satisfying their need for companionship and mine for money.

And just to prove my point to my Doubting Thomas husband, I asked Sylvia, "But it didn't bother you that Sid wasn't really my uncle?"

"Not really. Like I said, you've got *chutzpah*."

I tossed Blake a *so there* smirk. I knew what I was doing. After all, it worked for the twenty and thirty-something crowd, so why not the sixty, seventy, and eighty-something crowd?

"So what can I do for you?" asked Sylvia.

I inhaled a deep breath, uncertain how to begin. Although I thought I could do a decent job of communicating murder and mayhem on the written page, conveying such news to little old ladies was uncharted territory for me.

Sylvia tapped her index fingernail on one of the Mahjongg tiles. "Spit it out, dear. I'm growing closer to the grave with each passing tick of the clock, you know."

I didn't spit; I blurted. "Sidney Mandelbaum was murdered last evening." Then I held my breath, waiting for I wasn't sure what.

Sylvia waved my bombshell of a statement aside with the brush of a hand and an unconcerned shrug of her shoulders. "So tell me something I don't know. The police were already here. Interrupted my lunch. One damn cop came up from behind and startled the hoo-ha out of me. That's how I got this nasty stain on my jacket." She pointed to the smeared jelly. "Never been ogled so much in my life. Got every damn cocker in the place staring at my left boob for the past hour. And that includes the ones with cataracts."

I assumed she meant cockers with cataracts, not that she had cataracts on her left boob, even though I failed to notice any half-blind dogs running around Larchmont Gardens. They did have a resident cat that lived on the grounds, but from the way he stalked anything that moved, I figured his eyesight hovered around the twenty-twenty range.

Sylvia pulled a tissue from inside her jacket sleeve and swiped at the dried purple blob. "I tried seltzer. Only made it worse. I'll bet you can see this damn stain from clear across the Hudson. I wanted to go back to my apartment to change, but the girls insisted we start the game on time. Like they've got a bus to catch.

"Anyway, it better come out, or that detective is buying me a new suit. This is my lucky Mahjongg outfit, you know. Bought it back in the spring of seventy-nine and haven't played a game of Mahjongg without it since. Hardly ever lose, too. Drives stingy Blanche Becker crazy. At first I thought she had set me up."

"What do you mean?"

"Arranged the whole thing. Phony detective and all. I thought it was one of those singing telegrams, but it isn't my birthday. Even if it were, Blanche is too cheap to spring for a Hallmark card, let alone a singing telegram. So then I thought maybe she bribed a relative. Not because it's my birthday, mind you, which it isn't, but because she wanted to get me too flustered to concentrate on the game.

"Still, it wasn't until you showed up that I started to believe she didn't somehow have a hand in it. The woman would go to any lengths to keep me from beating her at Mahjongg. As long as she didn't have to pay anything. Did you know she comes from a long line of slumlords?"

I shook my head, at a loss for words and finding it difficult to keep up with her train of thought. Sylvia spoke as fast as she tossed Mahjongg tiles. I marveled at the lung capacity hidden behind what I estimated as a pair of 38D tatas. The woman rarely came up for air. I grew more depressed with each syllable she uttered. *Please, God. Don't let that be the future me.*

"The woman makes Leona Helmsley, look like Mother Theresa, said Sylvia. She finally paused and eyed me for a moment. "So Sidney's really dead?"

I nodded. "As really dead as Leona Helmsley and Mother Theresa."

"I believe you. You might have lied about him being your uncle, but you have an honest face. That's how I could tell he wasn't really your uncle. You're not a very good liar, you know, dear."

Seems I've been told that on more than one occasion.

She leaned closer and rubbed her hands together. Her face brightened. "So dish. How'd that dirty rotten scoundrel get it? And who do you think did him in? The detective refused to tell me anything. Asked me a bunch of weird questions but refused to answer any of mine. He kept muttering about not being able to discuss an ongoing investigation."

"He?" Blake pulled his attention from the ceiling tile and exchanged a quick glance with me. His had worry written all over it. I suppose mine did, too, considering the sudden clammy feel of my skin and two-ton lead weight that had settled in my stomach.

"Don't you mean she?" I asked. "Detective Menendez? *Loretta* Menendez?"

"Honey, my eyes aren't that bad and my marbles are all still rattling around upstairs, contrary to what Blanche Becker believes. Haven't lost any yet and don't plan to. I can still tell the difference between a guy and a gal, just fine. Even if the guy's wearing a dress and heels. Can't fool me."

My jaw dropped. "The detective was in drag?"

Sylvia made a *tsking* noise with her tongue. "Of course not. Where'd you get such a fool idea?"

"But you just said—"

"I know what I said, and I didn't say anything about anyone in drag. Don't put words in my mouth."

Blake apparently had studied the water stain long enough. He walked over to the table, took the seat opposite Sylvia and asked,

"Can you describe the man?"

"Of course. Huge hunk of a fellow. What in my day we referred to as built like a brick shithouse, you should pardon the expression. That's why I suspected a singing telegram at first. I was looking forward to him stripping down to his skivvies and giving us a bit of bump and grind."

She winked at Blake as she paused for breath. "Anyway, he reminded me a bit of Arnold what's-his-face. The one who married that Kennedy girl. Only she wasn't a Kennedy because her father was something else. He was in politics for a bit. Not the father. He's dead. Arnold. Governor Terminator, they called him. Out in California. Except he's not the governor anymore, and he got caught up in some sex scandal, and the marriage is kaput." She waved her hand in annoyance. "You know who I mean. Only the detective didn't speak with an accent. And his hair was shorter."

"Do you remember his name?" I asked.

Sylvia thought for a moment. "Kroft? No, that wasn't it." She tapped her index finger against her chin and stared at the ceiling. "Craine? Kroll?"

"Craft?" asked Blake.

FIVE

"Craft." Sylvia nodded. "Yes, Craft. Detective Craft. I remember thinking how suitable. You know, a crafty detective? Like Columbo. He acted clueless, but his wheels were always spinning."

"Crafty, all right, but he's no detective," I said. "Columbo or otherwise."

"Don't be silly, dear. I may be old, but I'm not senile. And I'm not stupid." She patted my hand in a way that made me wonder if she thought I might be one or the other. Or both. "I demanded to see his ID before I'd answer any questions. He showed me his badge."

"Yes, well..." I wasn't sure how to tell her she'd been duped. Like me.

Blake jumped in and explained the situation to Sylvia. When he was through, she shifted her gaze back and forth between us several times before finally saying, "Oh, dear. Looks like I've been had, doesn't it?"

"We both were," I said, this time patting her hand in

reassurance. "What did he want to know?"

"Only one thing, really. What Sidney and I discussed." She shrugged. "Anyway, I guess it doesn't really matter that he wasn't a real detective."

"Why is that?" I asked.

"I wasn't any help to him."

"How do you know that?" asked Blake.

Sylvia scowled. "My big date with that loser lasted all of five minutes."

Loser? True, Sid wasn't my idea of the perfect date—given his cigars and crude mannerisms, but he didn't suffer from halitosis or body odor. He didn't click his dentures or shoot spittle from his mouth when he spoke. His clothes weren't rumpled or stained, and he didn't wear a feed cap. Sylvia had not only given him her phone number, she'd accepted a date when he called her. As did most of the other women I'd introduced to Sid. I chalked it up to that old adage about there being someone for everyone. That and beggars can't be choosers, given the male to female ratio of the over-sixty set.

"Did one of you become ill?"

Sylvia snorted. "Not me. And he seemed fine until he up and left without any explanation."

"I don't understand," I said. "The two of you hit it off when you first met. What happened?"

"I haven't a clue. We were on our way to dinner. As we passed the solarium, I spotted Blanche and stopped to introduce her to Sidney. You know, show him off? Blanche never dates. With all the women around here, who'd be interested in that sourpuss, right?

"Anyway, Sidney says he needs to use the little boy's room, so I told him I'd wait for him in the solarium. Only he never came back. The man pulled a Judge Crater on me. At first I thought maybe he'd taken ill, so after about ten minutes or so, I asked Rodney Shapiro to check the men's room for me."

"Sid wasn't there?" I asked.

"Not only wasn't he there, according to Bert Goldfarb, who spends more time in the john than any five residents put together, he'd been alone in the men's room for at least twenty minutes."

"And Sid never called you?"

Sylvia shook her head and sighed. "Haven't heard a word from the man. Five minutes earlier he'd promised to ring my chimes after dinner." She sighed again, only this time deeper and accompanied it with a *tsking* noise. "Haven't had my chimes rung in ages, you know."

I glanced over at Blake. His cheeks had deepened to a dark rose, and he looked like he wanted to crawl under the card table. My husband is no prude, but I guess, like me, the thought of geriatric sex conjured up an image of our parents getting down and dirty. And who wants to go there?

"Besides," continued Sylvia, barely coming up for air, "I was looking forward to the key lime pie at Charlie Brown's. Haven't had a decent slice of key lime since my last trip to Miami back in January when I went to visit my daughter and that worthless husband of hers. I don't know how Charlie Brown's does it, but no one else around here comes close to Florida key lime."

~*~

"Now that was odd," I said as Blake and I took our leave of Sylvia Schuster and headed for our car.

"Not to mention a complete waste of time," said Blake.

"Not necessarily. We confirmed Craft is a phony. He can't be both FBI and a county detective."

"Detective Menendez told you Remick and Craft were imposters hours ago."

"And Sylvia Schuster confirmed it. At least we now know Menendez wasn't lying to me."

Blake glanced over at me. He had *The Look* planted firmly on his face. *The Voice* followed. "Why on earth would you think Menendez was lying to you?"

"I remember an episode of—"

"Gracie!"

"What?"

"Real life. This is real life. Not television. Not the movies. Not a mystery novel. Got it?"

"I have two words to say to you, Blake."

"And they are?"

"New Jersey."

"New Jersey?"

"Exactly. New Jersey. Home of unscrupulous politicians. Scandal and corruption. Cops on the take. It's a time-honored tradition. Besides, ever hear the expression, 'Life imitates art?' And what about 'Truth is stranger than fiction?' I think you need to stop being so logical and start thinking outside the box a bit more if we're going to solve Not-Sid's murder."

Blake chuckled. "And here I thought you wanted me around for my logic."

He had me there. "All right. For argument's sake, let's assume Menendez didn't lie to me, and Remick and Craft are definitely not FBI or detectives and definitely up to no good. What could that 'no good' something be?"

"Got me," he said.

As we waited to merge into traffic, a late-model black Taurus turned into the entrance of Larchmont Gardens. Looked like Sylvia was about to have a visit from Detective Menendez.

"So where do we go from here?" asked Blake.

I pulled out my list and scanned the names of Not-Sid's various dates. "Charlene Koltchefsky lives closest. Why don't we pay her a visit?"

I gave Blake the address. He punched it into our GPS, then headed back over the mountain into Scotch Plains. Ten minutes later we pulled up in front of a nineteen-sixties split-level, an exact copy of every other house on the quiet, suburban street.

Like many New Jersey neighborhoods, this one was probably once a family farm. New Jersey had become the Garden State in name only, even though the motto still adorns our license plates and road signs. Forget Jersey tomatoes unless you grow them yourself in your backyard. Even during the height of summer, most of our tomatoes come from Florida and California. The only thing springing up on Jersey farms nowadays are sub-divisions of million dollar McMansions.

Charlene Koltchefsky's forest green-trimmed, buttercup yellow split-level home sat behind a manicured lawn adorned with half a dozen birdbaths, a fuchsia gazing ball, and assorted gnome statuary peeking out from behind various low-lying shrubs. A twig wreath with purple and yellow silk pansies hung from the front door. Two yellow and green polka-dot frogs framed a welcome sign nestled within the center of the wreath.

"How much you want to bet she's got plastic slipcovers?" asked Blake.

"Shh." I elbowed him in the ribs before ringing the doorbell. "Your Aunt Fran has plastic slipcovers."

"I know," he said. "That's what worries me. One Aunt Fran in this world is enough."

From inside the house we heard someone yell, "I got it!" A moment later the door swung open. "Professor Elliott!"

Blake's jaw dropped.

I stared at the young woman staring at my husband. She wore a skimpy black lace camisole over a pair of low-slung black jeans. A gold hoop was inserted through her belly button. Three gold safety pins protruded from each eyebrow. A variety of hoops and studs ran up the length of each ear with chandelier earrings hanging from her lobes. Another hoop hung between her nostrils. A gold stud was set into the dimpled area under her lower lip; a matching one pierced her left nostril. Her spiky jet black hair was dyed vermillion at the tips. The color matched her lipstick.

And then there were the tattoos. Judging from Blake's reaction, this had to be Tiffany Robeling, but if so, how could Blake have forgotten to mention the tattoos? Images of roses, crosses, and barbed vines covered one arm from her wrist to her shoulder. A full-length portrait of Jesus ran the length of her other arm. Scripture emblazoned the exposed area of her chest, and angels with harps perched on either side of the hoop in her belly button.

Some people wore their religion on their sleeves; this girl had turned her body into a billboard to her faith. However, I'm guessing I wouldn't find "Thou shalt not steal" anywhere on her body. Or "Practice what you preach."

I glanced over at Blake. I wanted to ask, "F minus?" but I opted for a bit of diplomacy. "Is this Tiffany Robeling?"

"Yeah, that's me," she said, hands on her hips, her chin jutting out. "Who are you?"

Blake cleared his throat and I suppose the cobwebs that had secured his tongue. Ever the gentleman, he proceeded with introductions. "Grace Elliott. Tiffany Robeling."

"Elliott?" Her lip turned up in a sneer. "Any relation?"

"My wife."

Tiffany gave me the once over. "What do you want?"

I checked the address I'd written down for Charlene and wondered if I'd transposed the house numbers. "We're looking for Charlene Koltchefsky."

Tiffany turned accusing eyes on Blake. "I can't believe you're ratting me out! Jeez, Professor, I didn't think you were such a hard-ass. What's next? Hauling me off in handcuffs?"

"This has nothing to do with you," said Blake.

Tiffany stretched out her arms, grabbing hold of the woodwork on either side of the door, as if she thought we'd force our way past her into the house. "Then what do you want with Gram?"

"Charlene's your grandmother?" I asked.

She jutted her chin out farther. "Yeah, what of it?"

I wondered how a woman who cultivated garden gnomes and painted polka-dot frogs felt about a granddaughter who stuck safety pins through her flesh. "Is she home?" I asked.

Tiffany eyed Blake again. "You sure this isn't about me?"

"Not in the least," said Blake. "I'm as surprised to see you as you are to see me."

Tiffany dropped her hands to her sides. She didn't look like she believed Blake, but she turned her head and shouted, "Gram! Someone to see you." Then she motioned us into a plastic slip-covered living room. Behind me, I thought I heard my husband stifle a groan.

"You better not be shitting me," Tiffany muttered. "Gram'll toss me out on my ass if she finds out I cheated. She taught high school before she retired."

"I promise," I assured her. Tiffany flopped onto one of the plastic covered, gold crushed velvet armchairs, but Blake and I opted to remain standing in the spotless but overly cluttered living room.

Charlene Koltchefsky's living room looked like an indoor craft fair. An array of floral motif needlepoint pillows rested against the backs of the gold and brown plaid Herculon sofa and each of the three overstuffed chairs. Crocheted doilies covered the arms; knitted afghans were draped across the backs. Painted ceramic plates and figurines lined the bookshelves on either side of the fireplace. An enormous silk floral arrangement in a wicker basket sat on the coffee table, another atop the mantel. The end tables held an assortment of decoupage boxes, bowls of potpourri, and sequin-studded candles. Framed paint-by-number landscapes filled the wall behind the sofa.

Charlene bustled into the room a moment later. She wore a paisley print cotton blend shirtwaist dress in shades of lavender and powder blue. I think I remember Aunt Fran wearing the same dress on one of our visits and wondered if Blake was having the exact thought. I dared not glance over at him for fear of either or both of us breaking out in giggles.

Come to think of it, before she sold her house in Clark and moved to a condominium in Vero Beach, Florida, Aunt Fran had cultivated her share of assorted concrete garden fauna. Although, I don't remember any gnomes lurking among her hydrangeas and azaleas.

"Well, look who's here!" said Charlene. "I hope you've come

to apologize." Her mouth set into a line as tight as the silver blue pin curls covering her head. Something else she shared in common with Aunt Fran.

"Apologize?" I stared at her, wondering if she had me confused with someone else.

Charlene wagged her finger at me. "You know, young lady, in my day when a gentleman asked a lady out on a date, he picked up the tab. He didn't stick her with it."

I glanced at Blake. The shocked expression on his face mirrored my own surprise. Turning back to Charlene, I repeated her accusation, just to make sure I'd understood her. "Sid stuck you with the dinner check?"

"He most certainly did."

This was not the Sidney Mandelbaum I knew. Sid may have been a bit vulgar, but he certainly wasn't a cheapskate. At least not when it came to paying me. He never once complained about my fee and always paid up front. And in cash.

Charlene eyed me skeptically. "You didn't know?"

I shook my head.

She motioned to the couch. "Sit."

Under the circumstances, I didn't want to risk insulting her, so I took a seat on the edge of the sofa. Luckily, I'd worn a pair of taupe linen slacks and not a skirt since I eschewed pantyhose whenever possible, even in the dead of winter. And having once worn a pair of shorts to visit Aunt Fran, I knew the hazards of exposing bare flesh to plastic slipcovers. Blake took a seat beside me, but Charlene remained standing.

"I'm sure Sid just forgot his wallet," I offered. "He's a very generous man." I purposely referred to Sid in the present tense because it appeared this time Blake and I had arrived before Craft and Remick or Detective Menendez. Charlene didn't strike me as the kind of woman who would complain about the cost of a dinner if she knew Sid was now pushing up daisies.

She glared at me. "So you think all old people are forgetful?"

"I didn't mean—"

She held up her hand. "Don't bother. I had the same thought. At least the first time."

"The first time?" My stomach felt like one of her garden gnomes had taken up residence.

"You mean to say he stiffed you more than once?" asked Blake.

Charlene nodded. "I didn't think much of it the first time," she said as she paced back and forth in front of us like a school marm lecturing a recalcitrant classroom of students. "We're all getting old." She waved her hand in a dismissive manner. "Could happen to anyone, I suppose. And to his credit, your Sidney acted mortified."

"Emphasis on the *acted*," said Tiffany from her sprawled position across the room.

Her grandmother scowled at her. "I believe in giving people the benefit of the doubt, young lady." Charlene turned back to us and continued. "He made a huge show of patting his jacket and pants, checking all his pockets. Then he turned beet red and apologized profusely."

"So you paid for dinner," said Blake.

She nodded. "Luckily, when I was a young girl, my mother insisted I always take some pin money with me on a date. Just in case, you know? The habit was so ingrained in me that in all my forty-eight years of marriage, I never left the house with my dear George without a stash of bills in my purse. Never had to use them, though. Not until my date with Sidney Mandelbaum."

"And he didn't offer to reimburse you?" I asked.

"Oh, he offered, all right. Suggested we go back to his apartment, but I wasn't buying the likes of that excuse. I'm not a loose woman, I'll have you know."

I took that to mean Charlene believed in playing hard-to-get—or at least waiting until the second date—because I definitely remember her asking about Sid's plumbing. Everyone asked about Sid's plumbing.

"You should've taken him up on it, Gram," said Tiffany.

Her grandmother shot her a menacing look. "In my day nice girls didn't enter a gentleman's apartment without a chaperone. Besides, he promised to reimburse me on our next date."

"But he didn't," said Tiffany, speaking to us. "The jerk stiffed her again."

"Not quite," said Charlene. "He did remember his wallet on our second date."

"Yeah, too bad he didn't remember to fill it," retorted her granddaughter.

"Anyway, fool me once, shame on you. Fool me twice, shame on me," said Charlene. "I wasn't going to get suckered a second time. I've heard all about these geriatric gigolos. *Modern Maturity* had an article about them just last month. I'm not trading my pension and Social Security for a little male companionship, only to have the man up and leave after he's run through my savings."

"You tell them, Gram. Men are such jerks." Tiffany bit her lip when she noticed Blake glaring at her. "Present company excepted, of course, Professor."

"Professor?" Charlene turned to her granddaughter. "You know this man?"

Tiffany jutted her chin in my direction. "Seems Yenta the

Matchmaker here is married to one of my profs. Small world, huh?"

Charlene didn't answer her, but she did knit her brows together in a way that made me squirm.

"What did you do when Sid didn't have any money again?" I asked, wanting to steer the conversation back to our reason for coming.

"I walked out. Figured if he had to spend a few hours washing dishes, maybe he'd learn his lesson."

Blake burst out laughing. He reached into his pocket and pulled out his wallet. "How much did he owe you, Mrs. Koltchefsky?"

She waved him away. "You don't have to do that."

"I insist." Blake removed a wad of bills. Have I mentioned what a gentleman he is?

"Take the money, Gram."

Charlene hesitated for a moment before holding her hand out. "With the tip, dinner came to sixty-eight dollars. He ordered two highballs for himself, and I had a glass of Chablis. And we both had dessert."

"No need to explain." Blake handed her three twenties and a ten.

"I'll get you change," said Charlene, turning to leave the room.

"No need."

She hesitated. "You're sure?"

When Blake nodded, she shoved the money into the pocket of her dress and finally sat down, crossing her slightly angled legs at her ankles and clasping her hands in her lap. Charlene had prim school marm posture down to a science, despite her slightly gnarled fingers and not-so-ramrod-straight back. She looked like a woman who refused to let arthritis and osteoporosis get the better of her.

I can take a hint even when it's not given. Trying not to appear obvious, I reached into my purse, quietly unwrapped a chocolate-flavored Viactiv and surreptitiously popped it in my mouth.

Tiffany cleared her throat and speared me with an intense grunge-like sneer. "So if you didn't come to apologize for that creep taking advantage of Gram, why are you here?"

SIX

I turned to Blake, my eyes pleading with him to take over as I worked my teeth free of the chewy calcium square filling my mouth. He gave me *The Look*, but what was I supposed to do? Talk around the sticky glob and chance chocolate drool running down my chin? Swallow the Viactiv whole and risk needing the Heimlich Maneuver? He could at least show some appreciation. After all, I chomped calcium for him. He didn't want me to wind up with a dowager's hump, did he?

By the time Blake had explained Not-Sid's death and the subsequent events, I'd chewed my way through the Viactiv. I hoped both my husband and my bones appreciated the sacrifices I made for them.

Charlene's expression hadn't changed when Blake mentioned Sid's untimely demise. No gasp. No flinch. No cringe. I thought that was rather odd, but some people don't believe in showing emotion, especially in front of strangers, and maybe Charlene was one of them. On the other hand, maybe the loss of sixty-eight dollars was enough of an incentive for her to commit murder. A lifetime of reading the daily newspaper had convinced me that people kill for all sorts of bizarre reasons. And often a lot less than sixty-eight dollars.

However, I dismissed the idea of Charlene as a murderer as quickly as it had entered my mind. If nothing else, I doubted she'd have had the physical strength to bash in Sid's brains. Charlene was half his size.

Instead, I turned my attention to her granddaughter. Tiffany seemed rather indignant over the way Sid had shafted Charlene. Enough to kill him? Tiffany was one buff, tough babe. Definitely a kid who spent more time working out than hitting the books, which would explain why she lifted papers off the Internet. From the looks of her biceps, she certainly had the strength to whack Sid over the head before piercing his aorta. I wondered if Charlene was missing any kitchen cutlery.

I watched as Tiffany hung on Blake's every word. Was she weighing her options? Figuring out how much we knew? Wondering what we weren't divulging? Or was her intense interest in my husband for reasons that had little to do with murder and lots to do with Blake's sexy good looks?

I'm not sure which possibility bothered me more. Either way, despite her myriad tattoos and piercings, Tiffany was too much a femme fatale for my liking.

Charlene stood. "Sounds to me like Sidney Mandelbaum tried to scam one person too many. Did I mention he started talking about a real estate deal during our first dinner?"

"No," I said. "What sort of real estate deal?"

"One where he was getting in on the ground floor and asked if I was interested. I told him absolutely not. I don't invest my money in anything other than blue chip stocks."

"Do you believe he was trying to lure you into an investment scam?"

"You tell me."

When my jaw dropped over the implication that I was somehow involved in Sid's dirty deeds, she waved her hand to dismiss any defense of my good name. Then she brushed her hands together, as if ridding herself of any Sidney taint that still clung to her. "I appreciate your coming to warn me," she said. "I certainly won't be letting those two imposters into my home. However, I'm surprised the police haven't contacted me."

"They will," I said. "I gave Detective Menendez a list of all the women Sid met through Relatively Speaking."

Charlene's very thin, penciled brows arched toward her hairline. "All? Exactly how many other women were taken to the cleaners by that would-be gigolo?"

I cringed at the unspoken insinuation. "Mrs. Koltchefsky, I can assure you I'm not running a gigolo service. I operate an honest business. Sidney Mandelbaum always paid his fees to me on time. I had no reason to suspect he was trying to con you or anyone else. And as far as I know, he didn't behave that way with any of his other dates." Although I was beginning to have serious doubts in that regard.

She didn't comment but nodded as she ushered us to the front door. As we were about to leave, she stopped me with a hand to my arm, "A word of advice, Mrs. Elliott?"

"Yes?"

"You seem like a decent young woman. Perhaps you should consider a different line of work."

I didn't need to look at Blake to know what he was thinking.

"Don't say it," I told him after we settled ourselves in the car.

"Wouldn't dream of it." He started the engine. "But she's right."

I glared at him. "I told you not to say it."

Blake opened his mouth to speak but was cut short by a pounding on the driver's side window. Tiffany stood beside the car, motioning with her hand for him to roll down the window.

"Thanks for not saying anything to Gram about you-know-what," she said after Blake depressed the window button.

"You're an adult," he said. "What happens in my classroom is between you and me, no one else."

She nudged her chin toward me. "She knows."

This kid was getting under my skin. I decided to disarm her with a smile. Since she didn't know me, she wouldn't know the difference between a beatifically innocent smile and the smirk which crossed my lips whenever I fibbed. It usually took people several lies on my part to figure that out about me. Or so I'd always thought until my conversation with Sylvia Schuster.

"Sorry," I said. "I have no idea what the two of you are talking about." I patted Blake's thigh. "And we really do need to get going. Nice meeting you, Tiffany."

"Wait!" She leaned into the car. "How about I do an extra credit project to erase that F?"

Bull's eye. Blake was a sucker for students who wanted to do extra work. "What did you have in mind?" he asked.

She cocked her head and smiled in far too seductive a way to suit me. "What's it worth to you if I find this guy's killer?"

"I think we need to leave that to the police," said Blake. "This isn't some game."

Tiffany inched her face closer to Blake's and lowered her voice to a husky whisper. "Then why are you playing it?"

"What do you have in mind?" I asked.

Tiffany's eyes glittered like a little kid who'd just gotten away with filching the last of the Oreos from the cookie jar and managed to lay the rap on her kid sister. She answered my question but kept her attention focused on Blake. "I'm cool around computers. I bet I can dig up all sorts of stuff on this dude."

"I'm sure the police have equally savvy computer investigators," said Blake. "If you're serious about erasing the F, I'll assign you another paper."

Tiffany sighed. "Won't be as much fun."

Or as productive, I thought. At least once a week I read stories in the newspapers about hackers entering government and industry computers. These kids seemed to have skills the professionals lacked. Putting aside both my dislike and suspicions of Tiffany's motives, I asked, "What harm could it do? Why not see what she can find?"

Blake stared at Tiffany. "Because whatever she's thinking of doing is probably illegal."

She backed up a step and raised her arms. "No way. You think I'd risk going to jail for some dude who suckered Gram? I'd rather live with the F."

Blake wavered. "Promise?"

She leaned back into the car and crossed her heart with her index finger. "Swear."

I stared at her. Hard. Why did I get the feeling she had the fingers of her other hand crossed behind her back?

"I don't know," said Blake, wavering back in the other direction. "A man is dead. Even if you don't do anything illegal, you could wind up in serious trouble."

"So could you," said Tiffany.

Blake cocked his head in my direction. "My wife is already involved. I don't want anyone else getting dragged into this mess." He shook his head. "No. If you want to erase the F, write me a paper on television censorship in the nineteen fifties."

"Sounds boring as tofu."

"Then live with the F," said Blake.

"I can't. I need to keep my GPA up to maintain my scholarships." When Blake didn't budge, she sighed, her shoulders slumping. "Fine. How many words?"

"Five thousand."

"What! The other paper was only twenty-five hundred."

"Which took you all of five minutes to download, splice together, and print."

"Fine. Five thousand words," she grumbled, turning to leave.

Blake called her back. "Tiffany?"

She stopped but kept her back to him. "Yeah?"

"Don't bother trying to find some obscure paper on the Internet. I've read them all."

She threw her hands onto her hips and spun around, a smirk on her vermillion lips. "You really are a hard-ass hunk, aren't you?"

Without saying a word, I nestled against Blake's shoulder and placed my hand on the back of his neck as I stared at her. I wanted to make sure Tiffany got the message that he was *my* hard-ass hunk. And totally off limits to her.

"You surprised me," said Blake a moment later as we pulled away from Charlene Koltchefsky's home, her granddaughter standing in the street, staring after us. "Encouraging her like that."

"She might've been able to help us."

"But you don't trust her."

"With good reason. Been there. Done that." My husband spent too much of his career fending off the advances of aggressive coeds.

Blake chuckled as he stroked my thigh. "You do realize you have nothing to worry about, don't you?"

I leaned over and kissed his cheek. "Hmm." Unknown to Tiffany, she already had two strikes against her if she had designs on my husband. Along with hating cheats of any kind—academic or marital—Blake never could shake his childhood fear of needles. I needn't worry that he and Tiffany would walk off into the sunset with matching pierced tongues. And Tiffany didn't strike me as a woman who'd give up her human pincushion obsession for the love of a good man.

"Not that I want to tempt fate," I said, "but if Tiffany has computer talents that could help solve the mystery of Not-Sid's death, shouldn't we see what she can dig up?"

"No, we should not," said Blake. "We're not dragging some innocent kid into this mess. It's bad enough I have to worry about you receiving visits from thugs posing as Feds."

"Talk about jumping to conclusions," I said. "You don't know they're thugs."

Blake gave me *The Look*. "What else would they be? Encyclopedia salesmen? Besides, if Tiffany were that good a hacker, how come I caught her?"

"She didn't hack your computer. She copped a few papers off the Internet and cobbled them together. You caught her because you have a photographic memory and have read every word ever written on the subject."

Blake frowned. "Doesn't matter. She was just trying to wheedle her way out of that F. Anyway, whose computer would she hack to find info on Sid? We already know he's not who he said he was. Without knowing his real name, how could she find out anything that you or I couldn't find? It doesn't take a hacker to do a Google search."

Blake had a point, and Tiffany had an ulterior motive that I suspected had more to do with having the hots for her hard-ass hunk of a professor than erasing an F. However, she struck me as the devious type, totally untrustworthy but capable of ferreting out all sorts of secrets. "If she can help solve the mystery of Not-Sid, I think we should take advantage of that help," I said.

Blake shook his head. "I don't believe you're sticking up for a coed with the hots for me."

"I'm willing to put up with her if she can help us." For a limited amount of time. And never, under any circumstances, would I leave Lolita alone with my husband—no matter how much I trusted Blake.

Not that it mattered since Blake had made up his mind. If I wanted Tiffany's help, I'd have to do it behind his back.

SEVEN

"Where to now?" asked Blake, diverting the conversation away from Tiffany. "It's getting late."

I took the hint and consulted my list of Not-Sid's dates. "Kitty Pichinko lives in Plainfield. We can squeeze a visit in with her before we have to pick up Mr. Klingerhoff."

Blake muttered something under his breath at the mention of Mr. Klingerhoff, probably due to our destination later in the afternoon, but it was Kitty Pichinko's hometown that raised an eyebrow and put a scowl on his face. "Plainfield?"

"Not all of Plainfield has turned into gang-infested slums," I said. "There are still some nice neighborhoods." I rattled off the address as Blake punched it into the GPS. A minute later we headed west on Route 22.

Kitty Pichinko was one of several women I had introduced Not-Sid to a couple of weeks ago at a VFW seniors mixer in Cranford. Not-Sid always zeroed in immediately on the women with large casabas. Kitty Pichinko, although not much to look at, given her frizzy dishwater hair, crooked nose, and stocky stature, had the requisite casaba cup size. Not-Sid rarely looked past the melons.

Kitty lived in a neighborhood where fifty and sixty-year-old ranchers, split levels, and cape cods shared acreage with a sprawling two-story brick garden apartment complex of the same era. Although in need of some TLC, the neighborhood didn't qualify for slum status by a long shot. "She's in Building Three, apartment B," I said.

Blake pulled around to the parking lot at the back of Building Three. After hoofing it to the front of the building, we found Kitty Pickinko lugging a full bag of groceries up her front steps. "Mrs. Pichinko, let me help you with that," I offered, coming up behind her.

She turned to stare at me. Puzzlement clouded her features. "Do I know you?"

"Gracie Elliott. We met several weeks ago at the VFW mixer. I introduced you to Sidney Mandelbaum."

Recognition dawned. "Oh, yes." She handed me her groceries. "Thank you, dear."

I passed the bag to Blake as I introduced him. "May we speak with you for a few minutes?"

"I have to get my groceries into the fridge, but you're welcome to come in." She fitted her key into the outer door. Once the lock disengaged, Blake held the door open for us to enter.

We stepped into a foyer in dire need of new carpeting, a fresh coat of paint, and brighter wattage light bulbs. With only a few minor tweaks, the description might also apply to the drab Kitty Pichinko who wore a threadbare ivory cardigan over a faded coral polyester pantsuit that couldn't possibly have been fashionable even back in the seventies.

Two doors, one marked A, the other B, stood on either side of a central staircase that I assumed led to apartments C and D. Kitty turned right and slid her key into the first of three locks on door B. After disengaging each of the deadbolts, she pushed open the door.

The eye-watering, nose-dripping odor of mothballs smacked me full force. I tried not to gag as Kitty ushered us through a spotless but spartan living room, so devoid of personal items that it looked more like a circa nineteen-sixties hotel lobby, into an immaculate but starkly impersonal kitchen. The complete opposite of Charlene Koltchefsky's "more is better" decorating style, Kitty Pichinko apparently subscribed to the Mies van der Rohe philosophy of "less is more." Or more aptly in Kitty's world, perhaps the reigning decorating anthem was "least is best."

I glanced at Blake. Behind Kitty's back, he rolled his equally watery eyes and mouthed, "Make it quick."

Meanwhile, Kitty appeared immune to the stench. Maybe the mothballs had burned out her olfactory glands and tear ducts decades ago.

As she unloaded her groceries and began placing them in her refrigerator, I explained the reason for our visit.

"Oh, my!" she said when I mentioned that Not-Sid had died. "And he seemed like such a healthy gentleman. I suppose you never know when your time will come, do you? My dear Charlie went like that. Here one moment, gone the next."

"In Sid's case, his time came well before it should have, Mrs. Pichinko. Sid was murdered."

Kitty dropped the grapefruit she'd been about to place in the fruit bin. Her jaw dropped, and the color fled from her face. Blake took hold of her elbow and guided her into one of the circa nineteen-fifties chrome and yellow vinyl kitchen chairs while I bent to retrieve the errant grapefruit from under the table. After closing the refrigerator door, I grabbed a glass from the drain board, filled it with tap water, and placed it in Kitty's hands. She stared at it for a moment before taking a tentative sip.

"How did it happen?" she finally asked.

I gave her the Cliff Notes version, sparing her the gruesome details.

"The streets are no longer safe," she said, shaking her head. "I don't dare go out alone after dark anymore." She heaved a huge sigh. "I'd move tomorrow, but with the economy the way it's been...well, who knows how long I'll even have Social Security and Medicare with the way things are going?"

As delicately as I could, I explained how I didn't believe Sid was the victim of random violence. "I'm trying to find out if his dates may have some information that might lead to the identity of his killer."

Kitty's eyes narrowed. "Why on earth would you think I'd know anything about that man's killer?"

Blake placed a comforting hand on her age-spotted forearm and offered her an expression filled with the kind of comfort and understanding that makes women of all ages want to swoon at his feet.

Gracie bad cop. Blake good cop. Whatever worked.

"What my wife means, Mrs. Pichinko, is that perhaps Sid might have said something to you at some point that could be a clue. Perhaps he mentioned something about business associates, relatives, neighbors? Someone he'd had problems with recently?"

Kitty took another sip of water, clenching the glass so tightly that I feared it might shatter in her hands. "What about the police? Will they question me?"

"Yes," I said, "they have a list of all Sid's dates."

What little color remained in Kitty's face quickly drained away. She slammed the glass onto the table, sloshing water over the lip and onto the yellow gingham oilcloth table covering. "I don't want to get involved with the police. You tell them I don't know anything."

"I realize the police can be intimidating, Mrs. Pichinko, but they have to do their job. I'm afraid I can't keep them from questioning you."

"Then why are you here?"

"I thought if I spoke with you and the other women, you might feel more comfortable discussing Sid with me. I'm hoping you'll remember something that could prove helpful in the investigation. Do you remember any of your conversations with him?"

She shook her head.

"He didn't speak about anything personal when you went out with him?"

"He hardly spoke at all. And we never went out. He came over. We had tea. He left. I never heard from him again."

Odd. Not-Sid pulled a disappearing act on Sylvia Schuster and zipped in and out of Kitty Pichinko's life in about a nanosecond. Yet he took Charlene Koltchefsky on several dates where he either scammed or tried to scam her out of the cost of dinner. Maybe Not-Sid suffered from multiple personality disorder.

Before taking our leave of Kitty Pichinko I warned her about the phony FBI/detective duo of Remick and Craft.

Her eyes once again grew wide with fear. "Do you think they're the killers?"

"We don't know."

Kitty pulled a pad and pencil from a drawer in her kitchen table. "What were their names again?"

"Craft and Remick."

She wrote down their names.

"Remember," I reiterated as we stepped from her apartment. "Only speak with Detective Loretta Menendez. Don't allow two guys named Remick and Craft into your apartment, no matter what they tell you."

She waved the paper at me. "I'll remember. Thank you for coming, and I'm sorry I wasn't more help."

Blake and I gulped fresh air the moment we stepped out of Building Three. "No wonder Not-Sid only sipped tea and made for the exit as quickly as possible," I said.

"Or maybe his quick exit had nothing to do with mothballs," said Blake.

"What then?"

"Kitty Pichinko wasn't worth the bother?"

"She had certain physical features Not-Sid deemed important in a woman."

"Frumpy?"

"Sort of Rubenesque."

Blake rolled his eyes. "She didn't have the requisite *Rubenesque* bank account to match, judging from where and how she lives. I'm beginning to think your Client Number Thirteen was more interested in money than female companionship."

"What about Sylvia Schuster? She's living in an expensive senior facility. She's got to have money. Why'd he pull a disappearing act on her? He certainly didn't have time to learn her money is tied up in a trust or doled out by concerned family members or whatever."

Blake mulled this over as we hiked around the building to the parking lot. "I don't know, but something's definitely not adding up. Your Sid was up to something, something that got him killed."

As much as I wanted to, I couldn't argue with Blake's analysis of the facts we'd uncovered so far. Not to mention the appearance of two phony law enforcement officials. Perhaps once we'd interviewed all of Not-Sid's dates, we'd have a clearer picture of what he was really after and who dispatched him to Saint Peter's early bird special at the Pearly Gates Cafe.

~*~

Rudy Klingerhoff's children worried about him. Ever since his wife died last year, Rudy had settled into hermit mode. His three adult kids, deciding he needed female companionship to draw him out of his self-imposed exile, had purchased a Relatively Speaking gift certificate for him. After much arguing, Rudy reluctantly agreed to partake of my services to get his kids off his back.

However, Rudy refused to let me take him anywhere other than to bowling alleys. Rudy loved bowling, both playing and watching others play, either at local alleys or on TV.

As it turned out, this didn't prove as much of a problem as I initially anticipated. Thanks to my good friend Google, I discovered that New Jersey is populated with vast numbers of senior bowling groupies. Who knew little old ladies love little old men with big shiny balls?

So once a week for the past several weeks, much to my husband's displeasure, we escorted Rudy to Linden Lanes. Blake's dislike of bowling puzzled me, given the sport's deeply ingrained history in television, going all the way back to *The Honeymooners* in the fifties and continuing to present day sitcoms. Maybe someone once dropped a bowling ball on his foot. He'd never say. Anyway, while Rudy showed off his ball skills to the ooh's and aah's of assorted single ladies and various jealous gentlemen, Blake would head for the snack bar and frown at his laptop screen.

Not only is Rudy great at sparing a seven-ten split, he's also damned good-looking for a geezer. Cary Grant good-looking, complete with an athletic build, full head of silver hair, and black frame glasses. We've even had our share of swooning women (I now carry smelling salts with me,) but Rudy hasn't shown an interest in any of them. All Rudy wants to do is bowl. Then return to his hermit cave.

"Rudy," I said, after we picked him up later that afternoon, "if you don't try to show some interest in a few of the women I introduce you to, your kids will just purchase another gift certificate."

Rudy shrugged. "Fine with me. I'll get to go bowling more. They took my car keys away, you know. Can't drive myself anywhere."

"I think they were worried about your depression," said Blake.

"You think not having wheels is going to make me less depressed? They complain I never go out. How can I go out without wheels?"

Rudy had a valid point, but he'd have to fight this battle with his children. "Maybe they'll give you back the car keys if they see you're making an effort to socialize."

"Fine. I'll make an effort."

"Glad to hear that, Rudy."

Word of Rudy's good looks, single status, and bowling skills had spread throughout the area, and each week we arrived at the lanes to find a larger crowd than the previous week. Which is why I wasn't surprised to find one of Not-Sid's dates in the crowd of spectators.

As Rudy readied himself to throw strikes and Blake settled into a chair to grade papers, I approached Maureen Boland. Mrs. Boland held the title for the largest casabas of any of Not-Sid's dates. Unfortunately, they hung down around what would have been her waist, had she possessed a waist.

Like Kitty Pichinko, Maureen Boland wouldn't win any senior citizen beauty pageants. However, she tried to disguise her deficits with enough makeup for an entire chorus line of Rockettes and an overabundance of precious bling. I could pay off my mortgage with what dangled from her ears, draped around the many folds of her neck, and covered each of her beefy wrists and fingers.

"I don't suppose you're here to deliver my stock certificates," she said as I approached her.

Uh-oh. "Stock certificates?"

"For the initial public offering of Windergy. Wind is the new oil, according to your uncle, and was he ever right."

"You gave Sid money for a stock purchase?"

"Fifteen thousand dollars. Now I'm kicking myself for not having invested more. Windergy stock has soared a hundred and twenty points over the last few weeks. Too bad the rest of the market isn't following suit."

Maureen Boland would soon be kicking herself for an entirely different reason. She'd also probably dropkick me right out into traffic.

"Mrs. Boland, how about if you and I find a nice, quiet place to talk?"

"Not now. I came to watch Rudy Klingerhoff. We went to high school together. Did you know Rudy was the first and only Union High student to bowl a perfect game in the history of the school league?" She sighed. "And he's still just as gorgeous as ever."

"Mrs. Boland, I—"

"I had such a crush on him," she continued, staring at the man in question as she spoke. "But he was a senior, and I was a lowly sophomore. He didn't even know I existed. I heard his wife died. That's why I came today. Maybe he'll notice me now."

"We really need to talk, Mrs. Boland."

She pulled her attention away from Rudy and directed it to me. "If you don't have my papers, we have nothing to talk about. Tell your uncle to deliver them when he gets back from Aruba."

"Aruba?"

"That is where he said he was going on vacation, isn't it? When is he due back?"

I glanced around. Everyone else was paying attention to Rudy. I tried to catch Blake's eye, but his head was bent over his laptop. My mental yell for help failed miserably. I took a deep breath and blurted out, "Sid isn't in Aruba, Mrs. Boland. Sidney Mandelbaum is dead."

"Dead?" Maureen yelled loud enough that everyone whipped around to stare at us, even Rudy Klingerhoff. "What about my stock?"

EIGHT

Blake came running at Maureen's scream. He tossed me *The Look*, shook his head, then helped me maneuver her toward a booth at the snack bar.

"You have to get me those stock certificates," demanded Maureen once she'd calmed down.

I quickly explained the situation to Blake, hoping he'd devise a plan of action for dealing with Maureen Boland. I only knew two things for sure: One, Not-Sid hadn't purchased any stock in Maureen's name, and two, Blake wasn't about to cut her a check for her lost funds.

"I'm afraid we have no way of doing that," was all Blake said, falling way short of the mark.

Maureen zeroed in on me. "You're his niece, aren't you?"

I hesitated. "More like distant kissing cousins."

Blake rolled his eyes heavenward.

"I don't care how you're related," said Maureen. "You get yourself over to his apartment and find my stock certificates." She fisted her hands and slammed her sausage-like forearms onto the table. "Now!"

I tried to explain that I didn't have a key to Not-Sid's apartment. Hell, I didn't even know for sure where Not-Sid lived. He sure didn't live at the address he'd given on his Relatively Speaking application. That apartment at the Cedars of Lebanon Retirement Center had belonged to the real Sidney Mandelbaum, and he'd died of kidney failure two weeks before I met Not-Sid.

Of course, I didn't mention any of that to Maureen Boland. Instead, I took the chicken's way out and said, "I'll do my best." Which wasn't exactly a lie. Really. I was doing my best. My best to figure out who'd knocked off Not-Sid. Now I had double incentive. Not only did I need to find his killer to save my business, I needed to find his killer to keep from getting implicated in whatever fraud the slimy flimflam artist had perpetrated on Maureen and who knew how many other innocent victims.

Maureen didn't ask how Not-Sid had died. I guess all she cared about was her missing stock. I still had the murder hurdle in front of me. Along with telling her to expect a visit from the bogus duo of Craft and Remick.

To say she didn't take the news calmly would be one of my more gargantuan understatements.

"The killer probably has my stock certificates." She narrowed her eyes at me. "How do I know you didn't knock off your uncle to steal my stock?"

"Would I have told you what happened if I did?"

"That could all be part of your grand plan. You get me my stock, or I'll sue you for everything you own."

Great. I so wanted to worry about a lawsuit on top of all my other problems.

Just then whooping and shouting erupted from the spectators watching Rudy bowl. Maureen glanced up at the electronic scoreboard. "And now you've made me miss Rudy bowl a perfect game!"

I wondered if I could make it up to Maureen by reintroducing her to her high school crush, but one look at the scowl on her face told me I'd better not push my luck. What little of it remained.

Maureen leveraged herself out of the booth and headed for the crowd surrounding Rudy. I buried my head in my hands and moaned. "Why me? All I wanted to do was earn some money while writing romance novels. I thought I was helping people, but I've made a mess of everything. Their lives and ours."

Blake stroked my hair. "We'll get through this, Gracie."

"How? You heard her. She's going to sue us. We'll lose everything. And how many more Maureens are out there? We still need to speak with Mary Louise Franklin, Leila Raffelino, and Suzette Stephanovich. What if Not-Sid scammed them as well?"

"One step at a time, Gracie." He pulled me into his arms and kissed the top of my head. He couldn't fool me, though. Blake was worried. Big time. Otherwise, he'd be blasting me over my "harebrained" business scheme and how he should have forced me into closing up shop before I'd ever met Client Number Thirteen. However, Blake Elliott wasn't the sort of guy who rubbed salt in his wife's open wounds—as much as he probably wanted to right about now.

We huddled together in the booth, watching from afar as Maureen literally plowed through the crowd surrounding Rudy. "That's one determined woman," said Blake.

"That's what scares me."

Whatever Maureen said to Rudy didn't go over well. He

turned his back on her and immediately began chatting up another woman in the group surrounding him. Three of her together wouldn't have added up to Maureen. The woman was no more than five-foot-two and a hundred pounds. Her ginger hair fell in soft waves to her shoulders, and she wore only a hint of makeup. Maureen glared at them both, then barreled through the gathering and stormed out the exit.

"Interesting," said Blake.

"At least we know Rudy has discerning taste in women."

Rudy continued chatting with the ginger-haired woman long after Maureen had departed. When his adoring throng began thinning out, he escorted her to the snack area.

"This here's Veronica," he said. "We're going to get us a bite to eat. She's got a car. You kids can take off."

Would it be too much if I bowed at Veronica's Easy Spirit-clad feet? Probably so. But that's how I felt at the moment. I wanted nothing better than to hightail it out of Linden Lanes, rush home, curl up in bed, and not wake up until the credits rolled on this Wes Craven horror that had become my life.

As it turned out, I barely had time to kick off my heels once we got home, let alone burrow under a pile of quilts. Within ten minutes of arriving back at the house, Detective Menendez accompanied by two uniformed officers, appeared at our door, warrant in hand.

"My computer?" I asked as I stared at the piece of paper she handed me. "Why do you want my computer?"

"It's part of our investigation into the murder of our John Doe."

"But I already gave you all my files."

"Gracie, don't argue," said Blake. "Just turn over your

computer."

"But my manuscript—" When had I last backed up my files? What if the police somehow corrupted them? "Is it okay if I copy some files first?" I asked Detective Menendez.

"I'm afraid not, ma'am."

Ma'am? I didn't like the sound of that. When had I morphed from Mrs. Elliott to *ma'am*? Did they know about Maureen Boland and her missing stock certificates? Had she called the police and accused me of colluding with Not-Sid?

"Gracie?"

Blake, Detective Menendez, and the two officers were all staring at me, the officers stone-faced, the detective with annoyance, and Blake with concern. As for me, my feet had bolted themselves to the hardwood floor of my foyer. I couldn't produce my computer because I couldn't move.

"Gracie!" Blake grabbed my upper arms and shook me out of my stupor.

"Okay," I said, tugging myself away from him. "You don't need to manhandle me."

"I was trying to shake some sense into you. Get your computer for the detective."

"Actually, sir," said Menendez, "I need to retrieve it myself."

Blake led Menendez upstairs. I followed behind them, the officers following behind me. "When can I get my computer back?" I asked.

"When our techs are finished with it."

"Are we talking hours here or days?" I asked.

"Depends what they find."

"It's not like there's anything about Not-Sid that I haven't already handed over to you." How many minutes could it take for them to figure that out?

"We'll let the techs be the judge of that, ma'am."

There she goes with that *ma'am* again. Not good.

Blake and I stood in the doorway of our shared office while Detective Menendez helped herself to my laptop. Then she stepped over to Blake's desk and scooped up his laptop, which he'd only moments earlier placed there.

"That's mine," said Blake.

"The warrant stipulates all computers in the home, sir. We'll need to search the rest of the house."

If *The Look* could kill, Blake would be arrested for wife-icide.

"Do you want dinner?" I asked after Menendez and her posse left with our computers.

"Only if it's liquid."

Relatively Speaking was quickly turning my husband into an alcoholic. Yet another heaping pile of guilt for me to add to all the other guilt weighing me down.

"All your files are on the college server, right?"

"That's not the point."

"Then what is the point? It's not like they're going to find anything incriminating either of us in Not-Sid's murder or anything else. We'll have our computers back in no time."

"The point, Gracie, is that this little business venture of yours has turned our lives into something out of a bad reality TV show."

"What happened to 'we'll get through this, Gracie'?"

"We will. What remains to be seen is if we'll get through it with both our sanity and our bank accounts intact."

I suppose I couldn't expect Blake to refrain from dumping salt on my ouchies forever. After all, the guy's only human, and I'd certainly given him ample reason with the current mess I'd created. Still, a supportive hug right about now would have been nice. Instead, he stormed off back upstairs, and I headed into the kitchen to throw together a dinner neither of us would probably eat.

~*~

Three hours later the doorbell rang. Parents live in dread of two things when their kids aren't safely ensconced under their roof. One is the late night phone call; the other is the late night ring of the doorbell. Both always send chills up my spine. Tonight the chime shredded what remained of my already frayed nerves. I jumped, the book I'd been trying to read (with little success) flying from my hands and landing in the middle of the family room.

Blake reached across the sofa and placed a hand over mine. "Relax, Gracie. One of the kids probably decided to come home for the weekend and forgot to bring a key." He set aside his book and headed for the front door.

Did I buy that? Not for a moment. When had either of the twins last forgotten their house keys? Not since middle school. Besides, it was only Thursday night, and both Connor and Brooke had Friday classes. They wouldn't dare cut so early into the school year, not with a college professor father.

No, the Elliott offspring were studying in their respective dorm rooms at this hour, Brooke at NYU and Connor a few miles farther north at Columbia. Or so I convinced myself, trying hard to forget my own college years and what little studying actually occurred on any given weeknight.

I closed my eyes and took a deep breath to slow the gallop of my heart. *The kids are okay. The kids are okay. The kids are okay.* I silently repeated the mantra over and over again until I heard Blake walking back toward the family room. He wasn't alone, but neither was he with either offspring.

"Let me handle this, please," I heard Blake say just before he entered the room with Detective Menendez.

NINE

"Gracie," said Blake, "Detective Menendez needs you to go down to headquarters with her to answer some additional questions."

I didn't move off the sofa. My gaze shot back and forth between the two of them. Menendez looked all business; Blake looked all worried. I did my best not to freak. "At ten o'clock at night? Can't this wait until morning?"

"I'm afraid not, ma'am. Murder doesn't punch a clock. The longer an investigation takes, the less likely we are of solving the crime."

"Then have a seat, Detective. Pull out your little spiral notebook and ask away."

"I'm sorry, ma'am, but you need to come with me."

"Are you arresting me?"

"Not at this time, ma'am."

Not at this time? What the hell was the subtext in that statement? Visions of orange jumpsuits swam before my eyes, and I definitely don't look good in orange.

I studied Menendez from the top of her tightly cropped no-nonsense jet black curls down to her black-laced running shoes, chosen most likely for chasing down felons. In-between she wore a white button-down oxford shirt, black blazer, and black jeans. Unless a subpoena was tucked inside the blazer, I saw no evidence of one. No subpoena meant this was a request, not a command performance on my part. And a request meant I didn't have to comply.

"Then I don't have to go with you," I said. Anyone who ever watched an episode of *Law & Order* knew that much. As soon as she got me into an interrogation room, she'd find some way to confuse me, twist around my words, then slap me in cuffs and haul my ass into an orange jumpsuit. It happened exactly that way on every TV cop show I'd ever watched. Except sometimes the jumpsuits were gray, khaki, or olive drab.

Blake stepped between Menendez and me. "We're going to cooperate with the detective, Gracie."

I jumped to my feet. "I've been cooperating, Blake. From the very beginning. I voluntarily handed over all my records. I answered all her questions. I even called her when I uncovered additional information. And where has it landed me? Apparently, right at the top of her suspects list. Me! Hell, I've never even received a traffic ticket."

By this time tears streamed down my face. I'd officially lost it. But Blake was right. Refusing to cooperate would only raise more suspicions in the detective's mind. Rationally, I knew that, but how many people can think rationally when faced with an impending orange jumpsuit?

I swiped at my tears and took a few deep breaths, trying to regain my composure. "Fine," I said finally. "Let's get this over with."

Although Union County police headquarters, located on North Avenue in Westfield, is within walking distance of our home, given the hour, Blake and I drove. Detective Menendez, minus flashing lights and siren, followed closely behind us.

Once we arrived, I was led into a room that looked more like a set from *Bones* than *Law & Order*, probably because the entire building was only a few years old, and the interrogation room hadn't had time to grow a creepy patina from decades of hosting drug dealers, rapists, pedophiles, murderers, and other assorted lowlifes.

Blake wasn't allowed into the room with me. I was left alone for what seemed like a decade but was probably only ten minutes. Time has a way of slowing down when you're stuck somewhere you don't want to be late at night with nothing but bare walls to stare at. The surveillance camera mounted in one corner didn't help.

Neither did the painful hiccups spurred by a combination of my earlier crying jag, a bout of hyperventilating on the ride over, and a heavy dose of abject fear. I tried holding my breath, but the hiccups continued unabated. I could only imagine the entertainment my convulsing diaphragm and wonky glottis currently provided Union County law enforcement as they huddled around a computer monitor and watched me. I glared at the camera, hoping they all laughed so hard they'd wind up suffering through their own bout of hiccup hell.

Detective Menendez finally returned to the room, carrying a cup of water and a cardboard folder. She placed the water in front of me. I picked up the cup and began sipping slowly. It didn't help.

"Do these look familiar, Mrs. Elliott?" she asked, removing

several sheets of paper from the folder and spreading the pages out on the table in front of me.

I glanced quickly at each page, spreadsheets of financial records for the various women Not-Sid had met through Relatively Speaking. I shook my head. "No."

"That's odd, considering we found these files on your computer."

"That's impossible. Why would I have such information?"

"You tell me, ma'am."

"I am telling you, Detective. I've never seen any of this before. And enough with the *ma'am* already. If anything, I'm younger than you. Call me Gracie or Grace or Mrs. Elliott, not *ma'am*." I slammed my hands onto the table. "I hate being called *ma'am*!"

Detective Menendez narrowed her coal black eyes and knit her bushy eyebrows together. "We found these files right on your laptop, *ma'am*, not even buried in your computer or disguised under a phony heading. Right on the *home screen* in a folder marked *Client Date Financials*. Now, I want to know exactly what kind of racket you and the deceased were running."

"None!"

She leaned back in her chair and folded her arms over her chest. "I have all night. You're not leaving until I get some answers."

I looked down at the page directly in front of me. Even my math-challenged brain saw that something didn't add up. Raising my chin, I fought to keep my voice modulated. "Fine, Detective. I'll give you an answer. My answer is that I don't believe you found these files on my computer. I think you're bluffing."

She leaned forward until only inches separated the tip of her nose from the tip of mine. "Trust me, ma'am. I am *not* bluffing."

"Really?" I picked up the sheet of paper directly in front of me, the one listing Kitty Pichinko's assets, and held it up between us with the print facing her. "Someone went to a lot of trouble to frame me but didn't do his homework."

"What are you saying?"

"Have you interviewed Kitty Pichinko yet?"

"I'm the one asking the questions."

"I've been to Kitty Pichinko's apartment. Either you haven't been there, or you think I haven't. No way is Kitty Pichinko worth three point two million dollars. The woman admitted to me she can't afford to move out of her deteriorating Plainfield neighborhood. Neither her wardrobe nor her furnishings have been updated in over thirty years. Her television set belongs in the Smithsonian."

I placed the paper back on the table. I don't know if Detective Menendez believed me or not, but she looked totally pissed. After a minute of staring each other down, she scooped up the sheets of paper, stood, and left the room, slamming the door behind her.

Once alone, I realized two things: First, along with scaring the crap out of me, she'd scared the hiccups away. Secondly, she'd only placed six sheets of paper in front of me. Not-Sid had dated seven women.

Ten minutes later, Detective Menendez returned. "You can go, Mrs. Elliott."

"That's it? After scaring the crap out of me and dragging me out in the middle of the night?"

"You want to stay?"

"Hell no, but I would like some answers."

"I'm not at liberty to discuss anything further with you at this time."

"So I'm left with one of two conclusions, Detective: Either you lied to me about those files being on my computer, or someone hacked into my computer and planted the files. Which is it?"

"I told you—"

"You're not at liberty to say. Yeah, I heard you the first time. But computer hacking's a crime. How do I know my identity hasn't been stolen? Right now someone could be racking up thousands of dollars worth of charges on my credit cards. What are you going to do about that?"

She didn't answer me. Instead she opened the door and said to the officer standing outside, "Please escort Mrs. Elliott back to her husband."

Interesting how I'd gone back to being Mrs. Elliott.

"We need to cancel all our credit cards," I told Blake after explaining all that had transpired in the interrogation room. "And contact the bank, our broker, who else?" My head spun, trying to remember all the advice I'd read about what to do if you're a victim of identity theft. "Damn her!"

"Who?"

"Detective Menendez, of course. We've been cyber-raped, and she doesn't care."

"Don't jump to conclusions, Gracie. Just because she didn't answer your questions, it doesn't mean no one is investigating the hacking. If you even were hacked. As you pointed out, she may have been bluffing."

"I don't think so. You didn't see the expression on her face when I pointed out Kitty Pichinko's net worth. That woman was seriously pissed. The kind of pissed that happens when someone points out something you should have noticed yourself but didn't. And why are you defending her? Whose side are you on?"

"The side of logic. And we don't have to cancel our credit cards or do anything else."

"Why not?"

"Because, Gracie, other than an accounting spreadsheet for your business, none of our finances or any other personal files are on your computer. They're all on mine."

"Oh. Right." I mentally smacked my head, but then thought of something else. "How do we know your computer wasn't hacked, too?"

"Since there's no evidence that anyone broke into our house, your computer was most likely hacked remotely, probably through the Relatively Speaking website."

"I suppose that makes sense."

"Just to be sure, when we get home, I'll access our credit card accounts on my phone to confirm there hasn't been any illegal activity."

"I guess it's a good thing she didn't confiscate our iPhones along with our computers."

"Which woman was missing?" asked Blake, changing the subject.

"From the papers Menendez showed me? I don't know. I was so fixated on the page that listed Kitty Pichinko being worth three point two million dollars that I didn't look closely enough at the names on the other pages. By the time I realized one page was missing, Menendez had scooped up all the papers."

I closed my eyes and tried to visualize the other five sheets but conjured up nothing but blurred images. I did come up with a theory, though. "The missing woman has something to do with the hacking and possibly Not-Sid's murder. She planted incriminating evidence on my computer to lead the police away from her and to me. She's probably the person who tipped off

Menendez in the first place. Why else would she show up tonight with a warrant for our computers?"

"That's certainly a possibility," said Blake.

"Maureen Boland threatened me tonight. Maybe she's our hacker."

"Even if she had the skill, she wouldn't have had the time needed to create the documents, hack into your computer, and plant them."

"True. But someone else did have time. Someone who took an instant dislike to me today. And she professed to being good with computers. I think this is the work of your Lisbeth Salander wannabe."

TEN

"I want you to promise me you won't confront any of those other women without me," said Blake. "I'll be home by two. We'll go together."

"What about Little Miss Girl With the Dragon Tattoo?"

"I'll handle her."

"How?"

"I don't know, Gracie, but you can't just get up in her face and accuse her of hacking into your computer and setting you up. That's not going to accomplish anything. Besides, you have no proof, only a hunch."

Always the logical one, my husband. I tossed him a pout. "I suppose she wouldn't answer my questions, anyway."

"Of course, she wouldn't. Would you if the situation were reversed?"

Again with the logic. I didn't bother answering, assuming the question rhetorical. "Call me if you learn anything."

"I will."

Blake kissed me good-bye, grabbed his java-to-go, and headed off to campus. I decided to make an early morning run to Trader Joe's to restock our rapidly depleting larder in case our kids popped in over the weekend.

However, as I sat at a red light on Broad Street, a black Mercedes SUV with tinted windows turned in front of me onto Mountain Ave. Forget Trader Joe's. My gut told me this was the car that had parked in front of my house yesterday morning. Trust the gut, I told myself and hung a right to follow the driver. What did I have to lose?

Real cops might have noticed a tail, but the driver of the SUV continued on totally oblivious of me. He didn't speed up, didn't switch lanes. However, leaving nothing to chance, I slipped on a pair of sunglasses and an old Westfield Blue Devils baseball cap I kept in the driver's side door pocket.

My hunch paid off when the Mercedes SUV turned into the driveway of Larchmont Gardens.

The driver pulled into a handicap spot in the residents' parking lot, even though the SUV bore neither handicap plates nor a resident parking sticker. I continued four rows farther down, parked in the visitors' section, and watched as Remick and Craft stepped from the SUV.

Always trust the gut.

As the phony duo made their way toward the entrance of the Commons building, I tucked my hair up into the baseball cap to better conceal my identity, then followed them into the building. Once inside the lobby, I glanced around, spotting them just as they rounded the corner at the end of the corridor to my left. After sprinting down the hall, I ducked my head around the corner and spied the two men entering the solarium.

Cautiously, I made my way to the solarium entrance and stood off to the side, hoping to see them without them seeing me. I caught a glimpse of a broad back and buzz cut through a tall grouping of ferns and other assorted flora that screened off a back corner of the room. A seating area was positioned on my side of the greenery at a diagonal to the buzz cut. I made my way across the room and slipped into one of the chairs, grabbing a magazine to hide my face.

"I'm telling you, Ma, they're on to us," said Remick or Craft.

"Someone tipped everyone off," said the other. "Those old ladies aren't even opening their doors to us."

"Then you're going to have to find some other way to get in," said a female voice. "I want my money."

"You want us to break in?" asked the first guy.

"Do what you have to," she said.

"How do we know this guy really was Dad?" asked the second man. "You said he didn't look anything like him."

"That's because he obviously had extensive plastic surgery to disguise himself."

"Or he could be someone else," said the first guy.

"Are you insinuating that I wouldn't recognize my own husband?"

"It's been ten years since he skipped out, Ma."

"You didn't see the look on his face when that dingbat Sylvia Schuster introduced me to him. A moment later he disappears, and she never hears from him again. Don't tell me that doesn't sound suspicious."

"Maybe he got sick," said the second man.

"I'm telling you it was your father," she said. "I saw the birthmark."

"What birthmark?" both men asked in unison.

"You never noticed? Your father had a port wine birthmark about the size of a dime behind his left ear."

"Lots of people have birthmarks," said the first guy.

"Not in the shape of the state of Texas."

"Shit," said the second guy. "This would've been a hell of a lot easier if someone hadn't offed the weasel before we got to him."

"He had to have told one of those women something. Find out where he was living. Once you get his address, I'm sure you'll find something that will lead us to where he stashed all my money."

"But he gave that dating site broad a phony address. What makes you think he'd give his address to one of those women?" asked the first man.

"Think, idiot! He may have taken one of them back to his apartment. Your father always was a randy old bastard."

"Jeez, Ma, I really didn't need to know that."

"Then know this: We're talking your inheritance. I'm not going to live forever. That should be all the incentive you need to do whatever you have to do to find that money."

"All right, Ma," said one.

"We'll find the money," said the other. "We won't let you down."

"You'd better not. Now get going. I have a canasta game scheduled in a few minutes."

Over the top of the magazine I held so close to my face that the words all blurred together, I watched as both men hastened from the solarium. They never glanced in my direction.

A moment later Blanche Becker zipped her scooter around the ferns, clipping several, on her way to one of the card tables. While her back was turned to me, I dashed out of the solarium. I needed to find Sylvia Schuster.

"What can you tell me about Blanche Becker?" I asked after tracking Sylvia down at her apartment.

"You mean aside from her being a bitter old skinflint of a tightwad?"

"I mean everything. Yesterday you mentioned something about her being a slumlord?"

She studied me for a minute. "You're too young to be losing brain cells. You must remember. The story made headlines in all the papers and was on the news for weeks."

"When?"

She thought for a moment. "Probably about ten years ago. Give or take."

I laughed. "Mrs. Schuster, ten years ago my life revolved around raising two young kids while holding down a full-time job."

Who had time to read a newspaper or watch the news back then? Between cooking, carpooling, homework, laundry, and all the other trappings of motherhood, most days I barely had time to blow my nose. And that was with Blake shouldering his fair share. Of the household chores and family responsibilities, not the nose blowing.

Sylvia opened her door wider. "Come on in, dear. How do you like your coffee? I've got a fresh pot brewing, and I baked a pan of brownies this morning."

Never let it be said that I'd turn down caffeine and chocolate. Especially when I needed answers.

Sylvia's front door led directly into an open concept living area decorated with contemporary furnishings in a warm color palette of rusts, golds, and browns. The main portion of the room served as a combination living room/dining area with a granite topped bar separating the dining section from a small galley kitchen. A door off to the left led to the one bedroom. Family photos covered the walls and the shelving unit opposite her sofa.

"Sit," she said, pointing to one of the two wooden Windsor chairs on either side of a matching bistro table. "Cream? Sugar?"

"Cream, thanks."

She rounded the bar and poured two cups of coffee, placing them, along with a pitcher of cream, on the granite top. I moved them onto the table. Sylvia returned to join me, setting a platter of brownies, two plates, a knife, and some napkins between us. "So you want the scoop on Blanche."

"If you don't mind."

"This have anything to do with the dead deadbeat who ran out on me?" she asked as she cut two pieces of brownie, plated them, and served me.

"I think so, but I'll know more after I hear what you have to say."

"Hmm...you think Blanche had something to do with his murder? He ditched me right after meeting her. I told you that, didn't I?"

I nodded as I took a sip of my coffee.

"Said he was going to the little boys' room, but that was a lie according to Bert Goldfarb, who spends most of his day in the little boys' room. I told you that, too, didn't I?"

I nodded again.

"And he was killed the very next evening. I wouldn't put anything past Blanche. She's such a coldhearted bitch, you should pardon my French, that I'm sure she's capable of murder. That woman would nail her own mother to a cross if she found profit in it. And if her mother were still alive."

She grew thoughtful for a moment. "She couldn't have killed Sidney on her own, though. She would have had to hire someone. Blanche doesn't get around all that well anymore. Maybe if she dropped a few dress sizes. She can barely walk half a dozen steps on her own. Bad knees. From all that excess baggage she carries around. Anyway, given that she'd have to pay someone, maybe she didn't have anything to do with his death. That woman has trouble parting with a penny."

"What happened ten years ago?" I asked, hoping to get Sylvia back on track.

She broke off a corner of brownie and popped it in her mouth, then began talking around the mouthful. "First you need a little background since you never saw the story on the news back then. Blanche Becker's family made their fortune in real estate in the slums of Newark and Irvington."

"How do you make a fortune in slums?"

"Her father was one of those unscrupulous realtors who created the epidemic of white flight back in the sixties. He'd move a Negro family—they were called Negros back then, not blacks or African Americans—into a neighborhood. The whites panicked. Blanche's father bought their houses up at rock bottom prices. He converted all those single-family homes into multi-family dwellings and charged exorbitant rents. That man singlehandedly turned nice middleclass neighborhoods into slums almost overnight."

I'd heard all about the downfall of Newark from my own parents who'd grown up in what used to be a lovely city. According to them. I'd always had my doubts, finding it hard to imagine that such a violence-plagued, rundown place had ever been a vibrant middleclass mecca.

"When her father died back in the early eighties," continued Sylvia, "Blanche inherited all his properties. Her husband Sheldon ran the business. He was a hundred times worse than Blanche's father, probably because Blanche wouldn't let him spend a penny to fix up any of the properties. Many had no heat, no running water. Broken windows. Holes in the roofs. Imagine having to live in such filth and squalor!"

"Why didn't the cities step in?"

"I'm getting to that. They did. Slapped Sheldon with hundreds of violations, tens of thousands of dollars in fines. Instead of fixing up the buildings, Sheldon disappears, along with a reported twelve million dollars of Blanche's family fortune."

"And no one ever found him?"

"Not him. Not the money. Maybe he hooked up with D.B. Cooper or Robert Vesco. But it gets better."

"Better?"

Sylvia grinned. She was definitely enjoying herself too much. Going for the dramatic pause, she popped another piece of brownie into her mouth, then washed it down with several sips of coffee before continuing.

"The feds indicted Sheldon and Blanche for tax fraud. Sheldon in absentia. Blanche hired some fancy pants barracuda of a lawyer. He convinced the feds she was just as much a victim, but it took years and cost her a fortune in legal fees. Meanwhile, she still had to pay all those city fines and fix up the properties. She wound up having to sell her three homes—one here, one in Boca, one out in the Hamptons—and move in here. Not that here is such a bad place to be, mind you. It's one of the best retirement communities in the state, but it had to be a shock to her privileged fanny to go from multiple estates to a one bedroom apartment."

"I'd imagine so." Sylvia Schuster might ramble on and on, but her ramblings were quite informative. "How do you know all this, Mrs. Schuster?"

"Like I told you, it was a big flapping deal at the time. Even as busy as you were with a job and kids, I'm surprised you didn't hear about it. I'm sure you can find accounts on the Internet."

I made a mental note to Google Blanche and Sheldon Becker when I got home.

"And you might think all Blanche's problems had a lot to do with her now being such a prune-faced misanthrope, but from what I hear, she was always that way, even when she had all her homes and all her money. Not that she lost everything. I hear she's still got a few million stashed away somewhere."

"You know that for a fact?"

"Of course not. I'm not her accountant or priest, but you know how people love to gossip. Some of the other residents here knew her back then. The moment she moved in, the stories started spreading like red wine spilled on a white damask tablecloth. Anyway, after seven years, she had Sheldon legally declared dead. That's all I know."

Only Sheldon wasn't dead. Sheldon bought himself a new face and a new identity with some of that twelve million dollars and entered my life as Client Number Thirteen, one Sidney Mandelbaum. I'd bet my Fendi Zucca Baguette on it. The one with the black leather trim.

"So what do you think?" she asked. "Were Sheldon and Sidney the same sleaze? That has to be why he ran out on me. I'll bet Blanche had something to do with his murder."

"I think they were the same guy," I said, "but I don't think

Blanche had him killed. She was trying to find out where he'd stashed her millions."

"How'd you find that out?"

"That phony cop who questioned you? He's one of Blanche's sons. I'm surprised you didn't recognize him."

"I didn't even know Blanche had kids. She never talks about them."

"After you introduced her to Sid, she asked you how you met him, didn't she?"

"Come to think of it, she did. I'd already figured out Sid wasn't really your uncle. Told her you were a wing woman who'd introduced me to Sid."

Blanche or her sons must have done a Google search to find me and my company. Although I used a post office box as a company address, it wouldn't have been difficult to find my home address. We're one of only a handful of Elliotts in the area. They probably spent Wednesday devising a plan and purchasing the necessary phony police and FBI paraphernalia, only to discover via the news Wednesday night or early yesterday morning that Not-Sid had been murdered.

Sylvia chuckled.

"What's so funny?"

"I'll bet Blanche and her sons didn't take the news of Sidney's death very well at all. I would've loved to have witnessed that scene."

So would I. What were the odds that her scumbag husband would inadvertently wander back into her life one day and wind up dead the next day? If I hadn't overheard Blanche's conversation with her sons, I'd move the three of them to the top of the suspects list.

But why after all these years had Sheldon, aka Not-Sid, returned?

ELEVEN

"You need to tell Detective Menendez about the conversation you overheard," said Blake later that afternoon when he returned from class and I'd told him about my morning discovery.

"Already did." I thought about not contacting Detective Menendez, especially after the way she'd treated me last night, but knowing Craft and Remick planned to break into Not-Sid's date's homes, I realized I had an obligation to do my civic duty. Not for Menendez. For the women involved. I didn't want anyone getting hurt.

"And?"

"It's her problem now. I guess she'll stake out the various homes, waiting for them to show up. She doesn't exactly confide in me, you know."

What I didn't tell Blake was that Menendez reamed me out for not having called her sooner. I had waited until after speaking with Sylvia Schuster. To Menendez's way of thinking, I should have called her while I sat eavesdropping in the solarium. Right. With the culprits sitting directly behind me. Terrific plan. Not.

"Do you remember anything about Sheldon Becker's disappearance ten years ago?"

Blake thought for a minute. "Now that you mention it, I do have a vague memory of some guy from around here disappearing with a boatload of money. That sort of thing happens every few years, though. The guy usually winds up in some country without an extradition treaty with the U.S. Or it turns out he was whacked and the murder made to look like a disappearance by the person who really absconded with the money."

"I checked out Sylvia's story on the Internet." Not that I didn't believe her. I wanted to see if I could find more details. And some photos of Sheldon Becker.

"And?"

"Blanche Becker's two sons are named Peter Remick Becker and Jeffrey Craft Becker. Remick was Blanche's mother's maiden name, and Craft was Sheldon's mother's maiden name." Before Blake could ask how I'd sleuthed out that information, I added, "Compliments of Ancestry.com."

"Not too smart using their actual names."

"Maybe they did so to keep from forgetting their aliases. They don't strike me as the brightest crayons in the Crayola box."

I showed Blake some photos of Sheldon Becker I'd printed off the website. Sheldon of ten years ago looked older than present day Not-Sid. Or present day Not-Sid up until someone plunged a knife into his heart Wednesday evening.

Sheldon resembled the Pillsbury Doughboy, all paunch and soft flab around the middle. He sported Richard Nixon jowls, a quadruple chin, and bags under his eyes too large to meet airline carry-on regulations.

The recently departed Not-Sid had had the face of a middle-aged nineteen-forties movie star and the physique of a man who'd spent a good deal of time on a tennis court. All muscle. No flab. From the looks of him, Sheldon Becker's only exercise probably consisted of raising his fork to his mouth. "What do you think? See any resemblance to Not-Sid?"

Blake studied the photos for a few minutes. "If Sheldon and Sidney were the same person, his plastic surgeon did a remarkable job of transforming him. I see nothing to connect the two men."

"True, but you could say the same about before and after pictures of Michael Jackson before he died." I took the photos from Blake and placed them on the counter. "Anyway, not to change the subject, but I'm changing the subject. Did you speak to The Girl With the New Testament Tattoos?"

"I never had a chance."

"Blake!"

He held out both hands, palms facing me, the universal gesture for *Shut up and listen, Gracie.*

I shut up and listened, but I made a face to let him know he'd better have a damn good excuse. After all, his wife had been hacked, and I was a thousand percent certain the culprit was that tattooed and pierced little cheat.

"When she walked into the lecture hall this morning, I told her I wanted to speak with her privately after class."

"So why didn't you?"

"Because ten minutes into my lecture the police arrived and hauled her away. In handcuffs."

"Menendez?"

"No, some cyber-crimes division."

"I knew it!" The gut never lies. "For hacking into my

computer, right?"

"The cops who arrested her wouldn't tell me anything. So I called Detective Menendez. This must have been before you spoke with her. Anyway, she admitted that after you pointed out the discrepancy between Kitty Pichinko's lifestyle and her net worth as listed on your computer, she had the techs dig deeper. Sure enough, they found evidence of hacking which they traced back to Tiffany."

"That little bitch went to a hell of a lot of trouble to implicate me." She probably wanted to get me out of the way so she could sink her tattooed claws into Blake.

"If she's adept at hacking, it probably didn't take her very long," said Blake. "Once she got into your computer, she would have had access to your client files. From there all she had to do was fake some financial spreadsheets for each of Sid's dates and plant them on your laptop."

"That explains the missing seventh spreadsheet. I'll bet there wasn't one for Charlene. Tiffany would have wanted to keep her grandmother from getting dragged into a police investigation."

"Especially one where Tiffany manufactured and planted the evidence," added Blake.

"I guess it never occurred to the police that finding the information right there on my home screen was too easy. Anyone who watches any one of a dozen cop shows on TV would have known that."

"Maybe cops don't watch cop shows."

"Are you kidding? I bet most cops watch cop shows. They sit around yelling at the TV when the writers get it wrong, then discuss the errors the next day around the water cooler. Same for doctors and medical shows and lawyers and legal shows."

"And you know this how?"

"Because that's what I'd do if I were a cop, a doctor, or a lawyer. Anyway, you suppose I'll get an apology from Menendez? I deserve one."

"Don't push it, Gracie."

"I don't know, Blake. Seems to me, I'm the one cracking this case for her. Every break she's gotten so far has come from me. Maybe I should become a P.I."

Blake responded with *The Look*.

I still wanted to interview the three remaining women Not-Sid/Sheldon had dated through Relatively Speaking introductions. Blake tried to dissuade me.

"Knowing Remick and Craft are planning break-ins, I'm sure Detective Menendez has assigned details to protect each woman," he said.

"That's a lot of resources. With all the budget cuts throughout the county, do you really think each woman has a patrol car parked outside her home? Maybe they're doing drive-bys once an hour or so, making a loop between the women. If I were Craft and Remick, I'd scope things out and make my move between the drive-bys."

"That's sounding very logical for you, Gracie."

"Which is why you should have thought of it first."

Blake couldn't argue with that, so he reluctantly agreed that we should still visit the remaining women.

~*~

Mary Louise Franklin lived in a sprawling rancher in Fanwood, a tiny community sandwiched between Westfield and Scotch Plains. I'd introduced her to Not-Sid several weeks ago at the monthly Social for Seniors sponsored by the Scotch Plains Y. I was surprised when Not-Sid showed an interest in meeting her, given her relatively normal-sized casabas and lack of looks. However, now that I think back, Mary Louise Franklin stood out from many of the other single women in the gym that night.

"I should have suspected something right then," I said to Blake as we drove down South Avenue.

"Right when?"

"At the gym."

"Gracie, back up."

I have a habit of doing that, bringing Blake into the conversation in the middle of my thought process. You'd think after years of living with me, he'd be able to jump in with complete understanding of whatever the topic in question. After all, he's supposed to be a smart guy.

I caught him up. "Mary Louise Franklin didn't have the requisite looks to interest Not-Sid. There were plenty of other women that night more to his taste, but after scoping out the room, he zeroed in on her."

"And your theory, Sherlock?"

"Carlos Falchi."

"Who's Carlos Falchi, and what's he got to do with Not-Sid?"

"He's a designer. And a Carlos Falchi Python bag hung from Mary Louise's shoulder that night."

"You're losing me, Gracie."

"That bag sells for fifteen hundred dollars, Blake."

His jaw dropped. "Do you own one?"

"Of course not. I merely drool over them from time to time. But you're missing the point."

"There's a point?"

I swatted his arm but not too hard, given that he was driving.

"The point is that Not-Sid knows his designer handbags. He

wanted to meet Mary Louise because of her money, not her casabas."

"Casabas?"

Oops! I'd never told Blake about the casabas. "Not-Sid liked his dates with what he called 'large melons.'"

"He actually told you this?"

I nodded.

"Not *Rubenesque?*"

I shook my head.

"You know, Gracie, it's a good thing the guy is dead."

"Why's that?"

"If he weren't, I'd have to kill him myself. Why didn't you ever tell me this?"

"Because I knew you'd act exactly the way you're acting right now."

By this point Blake had pulled up in front of Mary Louise's house and parked. I jumped out of the car to put an end to the conversation. Not-Sid was dead. Blake didn't need to get all Sir Galahad on me, defending my honor after the fact. He should only know how many dirty old men I dealt with for years in the garment industry. No, actually, he shouldn't. And he never would.

"No police cruiser," I said, stating the obvious and changing the subject at the same time.

Blake grunted.

"And no garden gnomes," I added. "If we're lucky, we won't have to sit on plastic slipcovers."

Blake grunted again as he rang the doorbell.

"Why hello there!" said Mary Louise after swinging open the front door. "What a pleasant surprise. Please come in."

She ushered us into a living room devoid of kitsch and

indicated that we should sit down on a plastic slipcover-free sofa. The woman had taste. Expensive taste. The room, more showplace than living space, definitely shouted designed-by-decorator. And recently.

So did Mary Louise. From her expertly highlighted head of bronze waves down to the Alexander McQueen ballerina flats, complete with their signature gold metal skulls, on her feet. An odd choice of footwear for a woman in her late sixties. I wondered if Mary Louise sported any hidden tattoos or piercings.

For all her obvious money, though, Mary Louise Franklin lacked even an ounce of beauty. The woman had a face that would stop traffic. And not in a good way. For Sid, casabas may have taken precedence over other features, but no casabas and butt ugly? I should have known something was rotten in Sidville, but I'd been blinded by Mandelbaum Moolah.

"I've been having such a lovely time with Sidney," she said. "I'm so happy you introduced us. We're having dinner tonight in the city. Our fifth date."

Blake and I exchanged glances. "Then you don't know?" I asked.

"Know what, dear?"

I took a deep breath, not knowing what to expect after I relayed the bad news. "I'm sorry to have to tell you this, Mrs. Franklin, but Sidney died Wednesday evening."

"Oh, no!" she wailed. "Not my Sidney!" Huge mascara-laden tears cascaded down her cheeks and plopped onto her raw silk pants, leaving black blobs against a celery green background.

She raised her head and swiped at her eyes and cheeks, transforming her raccoon look into that of a coal miner. "How?" She snuffled. "Was it his heart? I told him he should lay off the caviar and foie gras. Between the salt and the fat, I worried he'd eat himself to death."

"The police haven't been here to question you?" asked Blake.

"The police? Why on earth would the police come here?"

"Sidney Mandelbaum was murdered," I said. "The police are interviewing—"

"All his acquaintances," broke in Blake, placing a hand on my knee.

I got it. This was not the time to blurt out to Mary Louise that *her* Sid wasn't a monogamous relationship kind of guy. "Yes, all his acquaintances," I repeated.

"No," she said. "I haven't spoken to anyone."

This struck me as odd. By now, either the real cops or the fake cops or both should have arrived to question Mary Louise. I had one more topic I needed to broach with the grieving woman.

"Mrs. Franklin, did Sidney ever discuss any sort of business deals or investments with you?"

"Of course not. Why would you ask such a thing?"

"I'm sorry. I didn't mean to offend you. I'm just trying to figure out why someone would want Sidney dead."

"I can't imagine. He was such a wonderful man. So generous." She released another torrent of tears, then blubbered, "He treated me like a queen. No, better than a queen. Like an empress."

~*~

"To quote Alice," I said to Blake after we took our leave of a very distraught Mary Louise Franklin, "curiouser and curiouser."

"In multiple ways."

"I'm finding it hard to believe that the same guy who stiffed Charlene Koltchefsky for a sixty-eight dollar dinner, not to mention trying to stiff her a second time, forked over the funds to dine on caviar and foie gras with Mary Louise Franklin."

"Apparently more than once."

"Maybe Not-Sid did suffer from multiple personality disorder."

"Or maybe someone is lying to us," suggested Blake.

"To cover up killing Not-Sid?" That made perfect sense, but I had a slightly different theory rattling around in my head. "Or maybe the liar is lying not to cover up her dirty deed but to protect the true killer."

Blake mulled this over for a moment. "Do you think the prim-and-proper retired school marm would lie to protect her granddaughter?"

"I don't think we can discount the primordial instinct to protect one's offspring. Or in this case, one's offspring's offspring. Tiffany expressed outrage at how Not-Sid had scammed Charlene. We already know she hacked into my computer and tried to implicate me in a financial scam. How much of a stretch is it to make the leap to murder?"

"I think it's a huge leap, sweetheart. You're suggesting every white collar criminal is capable of committing acts of violence."

"Who's to say they're not, given the proper set of circumstances? Tiffany certainly struck me as someone quite capable of killing, especially if she believed the victim deserved to die."

"But is her grandmother capable of a cover-up to protect her?" Blake shook his head. "I'm not buying it, Gracie. Charlene struck me as the kind of woman who would insist on Tiffany paying her dues to society."

"Maybe." Or maybe not. If someone wanted to lock up one of my kids, I'd do everything in my power to prevent it, no matter what. And as previously mentioned, I'm a law-abiding citizen who's never even had a traffic ticket. So who's to say how far Charlene would go to protect Tiffany?

TWELVE

From Mary Louise Franklin's home, Blake and I headed over to pay a visit to Leila Raffelino. Leila also lived in the borough of Fanwood but at Dakota West, an upscale condo community designed to resemble the iconic Manhattan apartment building from which it took its name. Only Dakota West was a scaled down version of the real thing. Still, the building was damned impressive.

Blake blew out a whistle after we drove down a long, tree-lined driveway and pulled into a visitors' parking lot adjacent to the building. I didn't know whether to interpret the sound as one of appreciation, envy, or a little bit of both. Neither of us had previously seen the newly completed structure up close and personal, although we'd seen photos in the newspaper. The photos didn't do the place justice.

A cross between German Renaissance and French architectural styles, the square building with a central courtyard sported gables, dormers, niches, and balconies galore. It positively screamed money. "According to sales I've seen listed in the paper, these babies start at just under a million bucks and go up to seven million. The monthly condo fees are more than our mortgage."

Blake blew out another whistle. "I'm betting Leila Raffelino received the caviar and foie gras treatment from your Client Number Thirteen."

"If she did, we'd have a pattern emerging. Not-Sid wined and dined the ones with money, stiffed middleclass Charlene Koltchefsky after she rebuffed his offer of an investment opportunity, and beat a hasty retreat from Kitty Pichinko's mothball abode."

We stepped from the car and headed toward the main entrance. "I wonder why he didn't dangle any investment schemes in front of Mary Louise," said Blake.

"I've been wondering that, too."

"Got a theory?"

"I'm working on one. Maybe Not-Sid saw Mary Louise as his Golden Ticket and had decided to marry her to gain control of all her money, rather than scamming her out of a small chunk of funds."

"Plausible but from the looks of this place, I'd say Leila Raffelino's portfolio makes Mary Louise's portfolio look like chump change."

"Unless Leila sank her entire portfolio into her new digs. Maybe Mary Louise has more in the way of liquid assets. What I don't get, though, is if Not-Sid was Sheldon Becker, what happened to all those millions he embezzled?"

"He probably blew through them," said Blake. "Twelve million dollars doesn't go as far as it used to."

I sighed. "I wouldn't know." Then again, neither would Blake.

"So you think he returned to replenish his depleted coffers?"

"That's one possibility."

"Not a very well-thought-out one. Why be stupid enough to return to the scene of his original crime? Wasn't it risky for him to return to New Jersey?"

"He obviously didn't think so. He'd changed his looks, taken on a false identity, even obliterated his fingerprints. What were the chances he'd run into Blanche, and she'd notice his birthmark?"

"He may not even have known about his birthmark. Blanche said it was located behind his ear. His sons weren't even aware of it."

"There were probably only two people in the world, let alone the state, who could have outed Sid as Sheldon."

"Two? Blanche and who else?"

"His barber."

Blake was certainly getting the hang of sleuthing. I smiled my appreciation of his Dr. Watson skills. "Still, why not target wealthy widows someplace where no one knew him, like Palm Beach or Palm Springs?"

Blake pondered this for a moment. "There's something we haven't considered."

"What's that?"

"Perhaps he deliberately returned to New Jersey."

"Why would he do that?"

"What if he hadn't been able to move the entire twelve million dollars out of the country ten years ago? He may have had to stash some and returned to retrieve the rest of the money when he ran through what he initially absconded with."

I didn't buy it. "Then why get involved with Relatively

Speaking? Why not just grab the money and dash back to wherever he'd been hiding all this time?"

"Maybe that was his original plan, but someone found his stash while he was holed away on some remote island in the Bahamas."

"So Not-Sid instituted Plan B? Find a wealthy widow to wine, dine, and wed?"

"Works for me," said Blake.

"Only we'd never know for sure because corpses don't talk. Or maybe they do but only to pathologists and forensic anthropologists like Temperance Brennan. And I doubt even Temperance Brennan could figure out Not-Sid's motives from examining his dead body. What sort of clues could she possibly find?"

Blake let loose a deep sigh, then tossed me *The Look* before we stepped into the lobby. I took the none-too-subtle hint and stopped babbling, even though I knew I was right.

Not surprisingly, Dakota West employed a security guard who stopped us the moment we entered the lobby. He gave us the once-over, his expression leaving no doubt we didn't qualify as future residents, even though I carried my mustard Milly Caroline Tote and wore a pair of Tory Burch wedges. This from a rent-a-cop who probably lived in Kitty Pichinko's apartment complex in Plainfield. He certainly didn't know his designer handbags and shoes.

"May I help you?" he asked.

"We'd like to see Leila Raffelino," I said.

"And you are?"

"Blake and Grace Elliott," said Blake.

Rent-a-cop glanced down at his podium, then asked. "Do you have an appointment?"

Appointment? We were here to see a suburban widow, not Donald Trump. "No, but if you'll give her a buzz, I'm sure she'll see us." I hoped.

Rent-a-cop picked up a receiver and pushed a button on his console. After a short wait he said, "Sorry to disturb you, Mrs. Raffelino. There's a Blake and Grace Elliott here to see you." He paused for a moment. "I see. Yes, ma'am." He hung up the phone and turned to us. "Mrs. Raffelino said this is not a convenient time."

Snubbed by a rent-a-cop! How embarrassing! Blake, ever the gentleman, muttered a thank-you, took my arm, and escorted me out of the building. I think he might have been afraid of what I'd say to rent-a-cop. Or do. If I'd known Leila Raffelino's apartment number, I would have stormed right past rent-a-cop and banged on her door. Too bad I didn't know which of the dozens of apartments was hers.

"Remind me where you introduced Leila Raffelino to Sidney," said Blake as we headed back to our car.

"TGIF."

Blake tossed me *The Look.* "I'm glad it's Friday, too, Gracie. Now, is there some reason you're refusing to answer my question?"

"Huh? I did." When *The Look* intensified, I realized Blake didn't realize I'd answered his question. "TGIF is a seniors' program at the Westfield Memorial Library on Friday afternoons. Well, not exclusively for seniors but geared toward them. They do allow people of all ages to attend. Although few do, other than seniors. I suppose because the programming targets seniors—"

"Gracie."

"Yes, Blake?"

"Do you remember what the program was the day you

introduced Client Number Thirteen to Leila Raffelino?"

"Of course I remember. I'm not going senile."

"And?"

"Something about financial security in tough times." I rooted around in my Milly Caroline Tote, and pulled out my iPhone. After accessing my calendar, I found the information on the TGIF event. "Protecting Your Nest Egg from Vultures."

"And you brought a vulture right into their midst."

I sighed. "You think Not-Sid tried to scam Leila, and that's why she wouldn't speak to us?"

"It's a damn good possibility."

I was quickly but reluctantly coming to the same conclusion.

"Would you blame her?" asked Blake.

I sighed again. Damn Sidney Mandelbaum and his Mandelbaum Moolah. I wish I'd never met the conniving con artist.

Only one date remained for us to interview. Suzette Stephanovich lived in another upscale retirement community, this one in Bernards Township. I hoped we'd have a better reception. I gave Blake the address, and we headed toward Rt. 78.

"She lives quite a distance from the others," said Blake. "Where did you introduce her to Sidney?"

"Not-Sid," I corrected him. "And they met at that reception for the Westfield Symphony." Blake had attended the event with me, but like all the others, he primarily stood off to the side while I chatted up the women Not-Sid zeroed in on for introductions. If he ever had to pick out any of my clients' dates in a line-up, he'd fail miserably. Blake accompanied me to these events with one purpose in mind: Keep Gracie out of trouble. He kept his eyes on me and no one else.

"Why would a woman who lives in Bernards Township attend a performance of the Westfield Symphony?" he asked. "It's hardly around the corner."

I shrugged. "Any number of reasons. She likes attending such events. She knows someone who plays in the symphony. She wanted to hear the guest performer that night. She has friends or family in Westfield. What difference does it make? She attended, and I introduced her to Not-Sid. That's all that matters."

"I suppose she has casabas?"

"They all have casabas. Not-Sid was all about the casabas." And apparently, the portfolios.

"Except for Mary Louise."

"Mary Louise's portfolio obviously out-trumped her relatively normal sized casabas."

Blake muttered something under his breath that I didn't catch and decided I didn't want him to repeat. Blake doesn't mutter often, but when he does, the mutters are best left muttered.

We continued driving in silence until we turned into a sprawling community of semi-detached red brick town homes. Only the painted shutters and front doors, along with the plantings in the small front yards and the variety of cars parked in the driveways, differentiated one from another.

"Doesn't look like Suzette Stephanovich has a Leila Raffelino- or Mary Louise Franklin-sized portfolio," said Blake.

Which didn't mean Not-Sid hadn't tried to scam her. "At least we don't have to contend with a rent-a-cop running interference."

"And judging from the car in the driveway, I'd say Suzette Stephanovich is at home."

Only how many women in their seventies drive humongous black Mercedes SUV's? From what I remembered of the diminutive Suzette Stephanovich, she wouldn't reach the pedals of the steroid-infused mega-monster parked in her driveway. "Blake, I don't think that's Suzette's car."

"Remick and Craft?"

"Maybe. Pull behind it."

Blake maneuvered our Camry to block Suzette's driveway. "Yes, that's the license plate."

"You sure?"

"Positive."

He whipped out his phone and started to place a call to Detective Menendez, but before he could punch in the first number, three Bernards Township patrol cars, their lights flashing, pulled up and surrounded us.

Three officers jumped from their cars, their guns drawn and pointed directly at us. "Step out of the car," yelled one. "Hands where I can see them."

"Do as they say," Blake told me. "Don't say a word. Let me handle things."

My knight in shining armor didn't have to tell me twice. I have a deep-seated aversion to guns, especially when someone is pointing one at me. And right now three someones were pointing three exceedingly scary-looking guns at me. I stepped from the car, my hands raised over my head, my legs trembling so much I feared I'd collapse to the ground. I glanced over at Blake. My unflappable husband looked anything but his normal unflappable self.

One officer kept his gun drawn on us while the other two first patted us down, then cuffed us. The pat down was humiliating, the cuffing painful. I think he purposefully tightened the cuffs to cut off the circulation in my wrists. I fought back the tears that stung at my eyes and stifled a whimper.

One of the officers, a thirty-something guy whose name tag read *Riley*, began reciting the Miranda warning to us. "You have the right to remain silent. Anything you say can and will be used against you in a court of law."

I turned my head slightly and started to mouth, "I'm sorry" to Blake, but two flashes of black behind his right shoulder caught my eye. Craft and Remick! They must have seen the patrol cars and dashed out Suzette's back door.

"You have the right to speak to an attorney—"

"They're getting away!" I yelled, pointing my chin in the direction of the strip of grass that separated Suzette's townhouse from the next group of four connected homes. "You've got to stop them."

"What are you talking about?" asked one of the cops who grabbed hold of my arm.

"The men who broke into Suzette Stephanovich's house. They ran out the back. I saw them."

"Nice try, lady. We've got our burglars right here."

"—And to have an attorney present during any questioning," continued Riley.

"No you don't," I insisted. "We pulled up right before you arrived. Your burglars are the guys who own that SUV, and they're getting away."

The cops looked at each other, unsure whether or not to believe me. Riley cut short the Miranda. "I'll stay here with them," he said. "You two check out these phantom burglars."

The other two cops jumped into their squad cars and peeled off down the street and around the corner.

By this time, a sizable crowd of senior citizen gawkers had gathered on the sidewalks on either side of the street. I hoped they all suffered from cataracts and wouldn't recognize me again. These people were my target market, but standing there in handcuffs, I wasn't the best advertisement for my fledgling business.

"Those aren't the robbers, you idiot!"

Blake, Riley, and I turned as a large woman exited the first townhouse in the group of townhouses next to Suzette's, the one on the other side of the strip of grass. She marched toward us, a Bichon Frise nearly buried in the voluminous sleeves of her pink and orange paisley caftan.

"I told 911 two *men*. I may be getting old, and my eyesight may not be what it used to be, but I still know the difference between a man and a woman." She pointed at me. "Does she look like a man to you?"

The Bichon yapped in agreement, its pink ribbon-bedecked head bobbing up and down.

"You called in the break-in, ma'am?" asked Riley.

"That's right." She bobbed her own head in time with her dog's. "I was watering the plants in my bedroom when that black car, that one right there," she said, pointing to the SUV, "pulled up into Suzette's driveway. Two men dressed in black got out and headed around back. So Fifi and I went downstairs to see what they were up to. They ducked behind Suzette's azalea bushes and pried open her bathroom window. That's when I called 911. They ran out the back door a moment ago and cut through to the next street."

Thank goodness for busybody neighbors! Whoever this woman was, I wanted to adopt her. "Any chance you could remove the cuffs now?" I asked Riley.

"Not a chance, lady. For all I know, you're accomplices of the other two."

That's me, the Fashionista Felon. Dressed in Ralph Lauren and wearing Tory Burch on my feet, I break into retirees' homes with the files and picks I carry in my mustard Milly Tote. I kept my sarcasm to myself, though, figuring Riley would take it as a confession. Besides, Blake was giving me *The Look*. I know when to behave. Sometimes. This was definitely one of those times.

Riley realized he hadn't finished Mirandizing us and started over from the beginning. "You have the right to remain silent. Anything you say can and will be used against you in a court of law. You have the right to speak with an attorney, and to have an attorney present during questioning. If you cannot afford a lawyer, one will be provided for you at government expense. Got it?"

Got it? I didn't think that was part of the Miranda warning, but maybe the courts accepted paraphrasing. Both Blake and I nodded.

A few minutes later Riley's radio squawked. "We've got them," said one of the other cops. "We're heading to the station. Bring in the other two."

Blake and I were escorted to the remaining patrol car where Riley held the top of our heads as we awkwardly maneuvered ourselves into the back seat without the use of our arms. Not an easy task.

"My car is still running," said Blake.

"And my purse is on the front passenger seat." I added.

Riley turned off the Camry's engine, grabbed my Milly, and locked the door. He pocketed Blake's keys and unceremoniously tossed my Milly onto the extremely cluttered and messy passenger seat next to him. I cringed, hoping Milly survived the greasy Burger King wrappers. I also wondered if he would have just driven off, leaving our car and my Milly for anyone to steal, had we not said something.

THIRTEEN

I've always had tremendous respect for the police. They put their lives on the line everyday to ensure our safety. However, I have no tolerance for stupidity, and right now Blake and I were the victims of the very definition of gross stupidity.

As we drove toward the Bernards Township police station, scenes from every law enforcement drama I'd ever watched flashed before my eyes. If there was any truth to any of them, I knew the drill. Once we arrived, the cops would lead Blake into one interrogation room and me into another. We'd each sit for hours in a hot, stuffy, windowless room while some detective tried to coerce us into admitting to a crime we hadn't committed.

I'd already been questioned by the police for something I didn't do. Let them pick on someone else for a change. Like the real criminals.

So imagine my shock when we arrived to find Detective Loretta Menendez waiting for us.

"Why are they cuffed?" she asked.

"We didn't know if they were accomplices," said Riley.

"They're not accomplices."

"You sure?"

"Positive."

"We caught them outside the vic's house."

Menendez turned to me. "Didn't I warn you to leave the investigating to me?"

"But—"

"Butt out, Mrs. Elliott. I have half a mind to let Bernards Township lock you up overnight to scare some sense into you. This isn't a game. Stop playing Miss Marple."

Miss Marple? I resented the little old lady reference. Call me Nancy Drew or Trixie Belden or Veronica Mars, but do *not* compare me to the septuagenarian Miss Jane Marple! She's old enough to be my mother.

Besides, if it weren't for me, Menendez wouldn't have a clue about Not-Sid's killer. Not that I had any clues, either, but I had uncovered Not-Sid's identity and Craft and Remick's plot to break into the homes of Not-Sid's dates. Which led directly to Craft's and Remick's capture. Exactly where would Detective Menendez be had I not butted in?

However, one look at Blake and I knew to keep my mouth firmly shut. No sense trying to douse a fire with oil. I'd wind up singed to a crisp, and he'd have every right to spout a few dozen I-told-you-so's. Instead, I offered the detective a contrite nod of my head.

Detective Menendez ordered Riley to uncuff us. He looked annoyed, but he complied. I don't know if a Union County detective can give orders to a Somerset County patrolman, but he didn't seem to want to test out any theories to the contrary.

Even though we hadn't been shackled for more than fifteen or twenty minutes, it felt like hours. Spasms of pain continued rocketing up my arms and shooting across my back muscles, after being freed from the restraints. My hands were numb, and red marks encircled my wrists where the metal had dug into my flesh. I shook my hands to get the circulation going, then rubbed at my sore wrists.

Riley handed me my Milly, now sporting a greasy French fry impression on one side, then reached into his pocket and tossed Blake his car keys. "You're free to go," he said.

"How are we supposed to get back to our car?" asked Blake, rubbing his own wrists.

Riley looked to Menendez for an answer.

"I can't take them," she said. "I need to question the other two you hauled in."

Riley grimaced. "Wait here. I'll take you as soon as I can."

~*~

As soon as I can morphed into *when I get around to it*, and *when I get around to it* looked like it might stretch into next Tuesday. After waiting half an hour, Blake called for a cab, but Bernards Township isn't exactly an urban mecca, and we waited another half hour before one showed up. By the time we retrieved our car and arrived home, it felt like next Tuesday.

Blake and I hadn't spoken to each other from the moment we left the police station. I've lived with my husband long enough to pick up on his moods. The thought balloon suspended over his head contained dark puffs of steam. I didn't blame him for being angry. After all, it's not every day a mild-mannered, by-the-book college professor is hauled off in handcuffs, but this really wasn't my fault. He had every right to be angry. Just not at me. However,

I don't think he saw it that way, and I was too chicken to broach the subject.

Our marriage has succeeded for so long because we provide balance for each other. I'm the Yin to Blake's Yang. Confrontation plays no part in our marriage. Or at least it hadn't until the day I told Blake about Relatively Speaking. Ever since, I've sensed a huge confrontation building, and at the moment, my tingling Spidey senses told me that confrontation was about to blow up in my face. So I took the coward's way out. As soon as Blake unlocked the front door, I made a beeline for the bathroom.

Five years ago, while still gainfully employed, I had designed a scarf pattern that became the next big thing, not quite along the lines of the quintessential Hermès scarf, but successful enough that the company bigwigs parlayed the pattern into licensing agreements for everything from clothing to linens to home furnishings.

As an employee, I didn't share in the big bucks they raked in, but they did surprise me at the end of the year with a bonus check equal to six month's salary. I deposited half the money in Connor's and Brooke's college accounts and spent the rest on a master bathroom redo, transforming our outdated not-renovated-since-Eisenhower-was-in-the-White-House bathroom into a spa retreat, complete with Jacuzzi garden tub.

At the moment my Jacuzzi garden tub called to me.

After twisting on the faucets, dumping in three heaping scoops of fizzing chamomile bath salts, and stripping, I settled in for a long soak. With any luck, by the time my skin pruned, Blake's logical brain would overcome the confrontational storm brewing inside him.

Or so I hoped.

However, as soon as the water filled high enough for me to turn on the jets, the bathroom door opened. "Go away," I said, my eyes closed.

"Not a chance. Hold out your hand."

Intrigued, I complied without opening my eyes. Blake placed a wine glass in my outstretched hand. I took a sip as he settled into the tub alongside me.

"We need to talk," he said.

I sighed. There was no escape, but at least I didn't sense any signs of confrontation in his voice. And he had brought me a glass of Moscato. Still, I responded by saying, "I already know what you're going to say."

"Do you?"

He laced his fingers through mine. Not what I expected. Maybe I didn't know what he was going to say. I opened my eyes and glanced sideways, seeing no angry slant to his mouth, no dark puffs of smoke in that thought balloon hovering over his head. Instead, I noted concern. And love.

I sighed again. "Maybe not."

"I aged ten years today, Gracie. I've never had a gun pointed at me before. Worse yet, I saw a gun pointed at you. Too many horrific scenarios flashed through my mind. I want us to live to a ripe old age together, rocking on the front porch, enjoying grandchildren, griping about our aches and pains. I don't want a future that includes prison, or worse yet, cemetery visits."

Neither did I. "You want me to stop investigating Not-Sid's death."

"Please?"

How could I refuse? I didn't like having guns pointed at me, either. Not that I wanted to play *Can You Top This?*, but I think I aged twenty years today. And I, too, was looking forward to grandchildren. Just not for a few years yet, given that Connor and Brooke were both still in college. Not to mention wanting miles of distance between me and any prisons or graves.

"All right," I agreed. Blake's logic had won out over my need to figure out whodunit and avoid any bad publicity for my fledgling business.

"There's one other thing."

"What?"

"You need to reconsider Relatively Speaking."

"I can't. We need the money."

"We need each other more."

My normally logical husband had let emotion cloud his judgment. None of my other clients were getting bumped off. Not-Sid was an anomaly. I saw no reason to fold Relatively Speaking over one scumbag scam artist who'd used me to get to rich women. However, this seemed like an ill-advised moment to launch into a defense of my business. Instead, I leaned my head on Blake's bare shoulder and dropped the subject. For now.

The shrill ring of the phone interrupted our relaxing soak. "Ignore it," said Blake as I reached for a towel. "It's probably a telemarketer."

Because the National Do Not Call Registry works so well. I often wonder if any of those nuisance callers ever really get slapped with fines and if so, do they pay them? At eleven thousand dollars a pop, judging from the number of calls we receive each week, the government should have been able to pay down the national debt several years ago.

Still, the call could be someone other than a telemarketer. "What if it's not?" I asked.

"If the call is important, the caller will either phone back or leave a message."

Practical as always, my Blake.

There are fundamental differences between men and women that have nothing to do with penises and vaginas. For one thing, the Y chromosome renders men incapable of multitasking, which makes women the superior species, in my opinion. However, that same inability to multitask allows men to ignore ringing phones whenever they're busy doing something else. Like watching football or soaking with their wife in a Jacuzzi. Women are genetically incapable of ignoring a ringing telephone.

So for the remainder of our time in the tub, while Blake did his best to distract me, my mind raced with worry over who had called and why. Men never seem to worry about such things. I haven't yet worked out whether that's a good thing or not, given that I have a tendency to worry about everything.

When the phone rang again less than ten minutes later, Blake gave in to my anxiety. He wrapped a towel around his waist and padded barefoot into the bedroom. A moment later he returned with the cordless handset. "Sylvia Schuster," he said, handing me the phone. "She says it's urgent."

Since the recently deceased Not-Sid was my only connection to Sylvia Schuster, an urgent phone call from her had to have some connection to Not-Sid's murder. And this is why women always answer a ringing phone. I took the handset from Blake and held it up to my ear. "Hello, Mrs. Schuster."

"I hope I'm not disturbing you, dear," she said, "but I thought you'd want to hear about what happened."

"About what?"

"About Blanche Becker."

I waited for her to continue, but when she didn't, I asked, "What about Blanche?"

"That lady detective showed up while we were all eating dinner. We had just finished our salad course. Baby greens with pears and goat cheese. Served with a champagne vinaigrette dressing. You'd love it."

"I'm sure I would, Mrs. Schuster, but what about Detective Menendez and Blanche Becker?" Once again, I shuddered to think this is what I might sound like in thirty years. Worse yet, is this the way I came across now? I really needed to make an effort not to babble.

"I was just getting to that, dear. As I said, it was just after our salad and before the wait staff brought out the main course. Flounder almandine with broccoli and sweet potato fries."

"Yes?"

"And that detective—what did you say her name was? Lorraine?"

"Loretta. Loretta Menendez."

"Yes, of course. Anyway, she arrives with two other officers and arrests Blanche. Right there in the dining room. Read Blanche her rights and hauled her away. In handcuffs. Made for quite a show, I can tell you."

I'll bet. I glanced at Blake as I asked Sylvia, "Did Detective Menendez say why she was arresting Mrs. Becker?"

That caught Blake's attention. He mouthed for me to hit the speaker button.

"Oh, she rattled off a long list of charges. I can't remember them all, but of course, there was resisting arrest. You wouldn't believe the stink Blanche made."

"Anything else?" The police wouldn't arrive to arrest Blanche

Becker for resisting arrest. That made no sense. They'd have to have a warrant authorizing her arrest for some criminal activity.

"I remember something about intent to commit something or other and conspiracy regarding something else. Anyway, that's not the best part."

"There's more? What else happened?"

"I'm going to be on television!"

"What?"

"I'm so excited. I haven't been on television since I was the original Karpet King housewife back in the fifties. I told you about that, didn't I?"

"Yes, but why are you going to be on television this time, Mrs. Schuster?"

"Because I was interviewed. I'm so glad I kept my hair appointment this morning. I almost cancelled it. Had a bit of indigestion, probably from the smoked sausage I ate for breakfast. I should know better, but it smelled so yummy, I couldn't resist a link. And you know how it is with sausage links. One link leads to another, and another, and the next thing I knew, I'd eaten three links. Of course, I immediately regretted my lack of self-control, but by that time, it was too late."

I sighed, noticing Blake's pained expression and quadrupled my resolve to dial down my own ditziness. If that was even possible. I hoped so because I definitely didn't want to grow into a Sylvia Schuster in my old age. "Who interviewed you, Mrs. Schuster?"

"That adorable hunk of a reporter with the blond hair, the one from Fox News. He arrived in one of their news vans and brought a cameraman with him."

"When was this?"

"Shortly after Blanche's arrest. He interviewed me for the ten o'clock news. I told him all about how you found Sidney Mandelbaum's body and how between us, we figured out that Sidney was really Sheldon Becker."

Between us?

"Only Fox News showed up? No other networks?" One was bad enough, but it seemed odd to me that only Fox showed up when reporters seem to travel in packs. On any given day, the same news story will break at the same time on each of the four major networks, plus cable.

"Well, I can't give an exclusive interview to all the networks, now can I? That wouldn't be ethical."

Exclusive interview? A huge boulder of dread settled in my stomach. "Do you know how Fox News learned about Blanche's arrest, Mrs. Schuster?"

"Why I called them, of course! This could be my big break to get back into show business."

How a news interview might result in a renewed television career for the former Karpet King housewife was too bizarre for even me to comprehend. However, I'm sure Sylvia Schuster found the step from Point A to Point B quite logical. Even if no one else would.

"But I wasn't thinking just of myself, mind you, she continued."

"What do you mean?"

"I believe in sharing the bounty with people I like, and I've taken a liking to you, dear. This could be your big break, too."

"In what way?" I foresaw only disaster coming out of Relatively Speaking tied to the Becker scandal, past and present.

"That reporter—I wish I could remember his name, Dan

something, I believe. Or Don? Anyway, when I told him about you, he said he'd like to interview you, too, and I thought that was a wonderful idea, don't you? He's on his way over right now. I figured you'd want to know so you can powder your nose and apply a fresh coat of lipstick."

That's when the doorbell rang.

FOURTEEN

I hung up from Sylvia Schuster and grabbed for Blake's bare arm. "Don't answer the door."

He glanced at the towel wrapped around his waist. "Trust me, Gracie, I'm not answering the door."

I stepped from the tub and began to towel myself dry. Damn Sylvia Schuster and her big mouth! "Looks like you'll get your wish," I told Blake.

"What wish is that?"

"The death of Relatively Speaking."

He offered me a noncommittal shrug. "They say all publicity is good publicity."

"I don't think that applies to having your business mentioned in the same breath with murder. By ten o-five tonight I probably won't have a business."

Blake had the decency to contain his joy. I glanced longingly at my spa bathroom and sighed, doubtful that any apartment above an auto repair shop in Newark would come with a Jacuzzi garden tub and a steam shower.

Blake threw on his robe and headed for one of the front bedroom windows while I slipped into my favorite Mickey Mouse jersey pajamas. "Looks like they plan to stick around for a while. They're setting up lights."

"How long do you think they'll stay?"

"Until they get their story."

"Do you think they plan to camp out on our street all night?" What would the neighbors think?

"At least until the news airs later. If they don't get what they came for tonight, they might show up again first thing tomorrow morning unless a bigger story breaks and pulls them away."

Was I wrong to hope for disaster to strike someone else overnight? Of course, not wanting bad Karma to come crashing down on me, I didn't wish harm to anyone undeserving of a massive dose of caca. However, there had to be some terrorists, rapists, or murderers lurking out there in need of capture and comeuppance. Not-Sid's murderer certainly came to mind. But if not him, someone who'd draw the attention of every network news van, including the one currently camped out in front of my house. Was that asking too much?

"You think the other networks will show up, too?"

"Eventually. Sheldon Becker's disappearance ten years ago was a big story."

Not that I remembered any of it. I groaned, and my body groaned along with me. Or more accurately, rumbled, reminding me Blake and I hadn't eaten dinner yet. Not that I felt like eating, but tell that to my stomach. And my husband, whose stomach chose that moment to echo mine. But I didn't want to turn on any lights downstairs. "How do you feel about cheese and crackers and grapes for dinner?" I asked Blake.

"Are the cupboards that bare?"

"No, but I don't want to risk setting the house on fire by cooking in the dark."

"Wise move. Although you do realize we could turn on some lights."

"But then they'd know we're home."

"It's our home, Gracie. We don't have to open the door to everyone who knocks. Then again, we might get them to leave sooner if you just tell them you have no comment."

I shook my head. "Not a chance. Haven't you ever noticed how guilty people who do that come across on camera?"

"Have it your way. A dinner of cheese, crackers, and grapes by the light of the moon is fine with me."

Blake stepped into a pair of blue and gray plaid flannel drawstring pants and pulled a gray Kean Cougars sweatshirt over his head. Together we made our way down the dark staircase and into the equally dark kitchen.

When I opened the refrigerator, light flooded the room. I quickly yanked out an assortment of cheeses and the bowl of grapes, then slammed the refrigerator door. Even though the kitchen was situated at the back of the house and no one out front would see the light, the reporter or one of his cohorts might be lurking at the back door. I held my breath, waiting for a knock. After the kitchen clock ticked away five, ten, then fifteen seconds without a rap on the door, I allowed myself to breathe again.

Until a few minutes later when I heard the front door open and I nearly choked on a grape.

"Like I said, dude. My parents are probably out to dinner somewhere."

"What do you know about your mother's involvement in the murder of Sheldon Becker?"

"What?!" This from Brooke.

"Who the hell is Sheldon Becker?" asked Connor.

"Your mother knew him as Sidney Mandelbaum. He was one of her clients. By the way, exactly what sort of dating service does your mother run?"

"What the hell are you implying?"

"Get that camera out of my face," said Brooke.

"I'm just looking for a statement from Grace Elliott. Mind if I wait inside for her?"

"Hell, no," said Connor. "Get out."

"Hey, hands off the camera!"

"Then stop trying to worm your ass and your camera into our house. Get off our property."

"And don't you dare put any footage of us on air," said Brooke. "You don't have our permission. Nothing we said is on the record. We'll sue."

The door slammed.

"What the hell was that?" asked Brooke.

"Beats me," said Connor. "I guess we should call mom and dad to find out what's going on."

"No need," called out Blake.

We heard Brooke and Connor make their way down the hall toward the kitchen. "What are you guys doing sitting in the dark?" asked Brooke, flipping the overhead light switch.

"Turn off the light!" I yelled.

"That's no longer necessary, Gracie," said Blake. "They know the kids are here."

"I suppose."

"So why are you sitting in the dark?" repeated Brooke.

"We're avoiding the vultures that just swarmed all over you," I said.

"About that," said Connor. "What gives, Mom? That reporter dude—"

"You mean sleazy tabloid creep," said Brooke. "No legitimate reporter would try to force his way into someone's home."

"He claims you have some involvement in a murder," continued Connor.

"Your father and I found the body."

"Holy shit!"

"There's nothing holy about shit," said Blake. "Sit down, and we'll explain what's going on."

"Can we eat while you explain?" asked Connor. "I'm starving."

"Of course you are." My eighteen-year-old son hadn't stopped eating since the day he was born, yet he didn't have an ounce of fat on his six-foot frame. I wish I had his metabolism. So did his twin sister who, unfortunately, had inherited my metabolism and ran three miles a day in order to maintain her size four figure.

I pulled out the Panini maker and began assembling sandwiches while Blake caught the twins up on events of the last few days.

"And here we came home for the weekend because we thought you'd be suffering from empty nest syndrome," said Connor. He laughed. "Looks like you've been keeping plenty busy enough without us, Mom."

Brooke punched him in the arm.

"Ouch! What's that for?"

"Your insensitivity, Dork Head!" Then she turned to me. "So you've like helped solve this case so far?"

"Your mother stumbled upon evidence she's turned over to the police," said Blake. "She's not working with them to help solve the case."

"That reporter made it sound like Mom had something to do with the guy's murder," said Brooke. "I've got a good mind to march out there and set him straight!"

Our daughter never met an injustice she didn't feel compelled to correct. From the time she was old enough to raise her tiny fists, she became the defender of the meek and trod-upon, a pint-sized crusader, feared by playground bullies everywhere. Both Blake and I believed someday she'd become President, making us the First Parents and her economics majoring brother Secretary of the Treasury. But only if he ever, in her opinion, matured beyond Dork Head status.

"You'll do nothing of the sort," Blake warned her. "No one is saying another word to any reporter. Got it?"

They both agreed. Reluctantly.

~*~

For the first time in the history of the Elliott household, a devoted *ABC World News* family going back to Peter Jennings days, we huddled around the television to watch Fox News that night. The news van remained parked in front of our house, but the reporter had made no further attempts to contact me, probably because he didn't realize I was in the house.

Would Brooke's threat about a lawsuit make him think twice about airing whatever the cameraman had captured of the twins? "Do you know for a fact they can't broadcast anything without permission?" I asked her. Perhaps she'd learned that from one of her poli-sci classes.

She shrugged. "I haven't a clue. Hopefully, neither does that reporter."

"Don't count on it," said Blake. "I'm sure all reporters are well versed in journalistic legal issues. Whether they abide by the letter of the law, is another matter."

The news led off with a breaking story about an overturned prison van on the New Jersey Turnpike near the Meadowlands. The resulting twelve-car pile-up included four fatalities. Two prisoners had escaped. The news chopper hovered overhead, focusing on a body bag at the side of the road. A police copter flooded the adjoining swamp with light as patrols with search dogs combed the area.

An involuntary shiver coursed through my body.

"Cold?" asked Blake.

I shook my head. "I wished for something awful to happen to divert the news media from me."

Connor laughed. "You do know you don't have that kind of power, right, Mom?"

"Of course, I know that. It still creeps me out." I hoped the dead were all convicts who committed heinous crimes and not innocent commuters unlucky enough to be at the wrong spot on the turnpike at the wrong time.

After a commercial break, the second news story dealt with a drug bust in Newark where cops exchanged fire with a dealer and a dozen members of his crew. Two officers were wounded in the exchange, one seriously. Because I'm good at rationalizing, I convinced myself he was a dirty cop, taking kickbacks from the dealer.

Another commercial break. Then the entertainment report, which dealt with some former child star arrested for DUI—for the third time.

"Three strikes and you're out," said Connor. "She's gonna do some time."

"Or land a reality TV gig," said Blake, grumbling about the new normal regarding celebrities behaving badly and the state of television programming.

"I hope not," I said. "Maybe sitting in a jail cell will scare her straight."

"Yeah, that's worked so well for all the others," said Brooke.

After yet another series of commercials, the broadcast moved on to the weather, then sports. Blake clicked off the television.

"Nothing about us or Mom," said Connor. He glanced out the window. "The van's gone."

"Good," I said. "Although I do feel sorry for Sylvia Schuster. She's going to be very disappointed her interview didn't air."

"She'll survive," said Blake.

"Still, who would have thought that a drunken starlet's DUI would trump the return and murder of the elusive Sheldon Becker?" I asked.

"It's all about ratings," said Blake. "Compared to the sensationalism of prisoner escapes, drug shootouts, and out-of-control celebrities, Sheldon Becker is an ancient story no twenty-something news producer would devote air time to, even if he did wind up returning to New Jersey and getting himself killed. A former child star arrested a third time for DUI? That's what drives ratings these days."

"So you think they won't air the interview with Sylvia at all?" I asked.

"Someone at the station made the decision to pull the story tonight," said Blake. "Probably because a speculative interview with a senior citizen wasn't deemed newsworthy enough, especially since the reporter couldn't nail an interview with you."

"Which means he might show up again tomorrow."

"There's also another possibility," added Blake. "Maybe they weren't able to confirm that Sheldon Becker is really dead."

"Of course he's dead," I said. "We found his body."

"We found Sidney Mandelbaum's body," said Blake. "We only have Blanche Becker's word that Sidney was really Sheldon. What if she was wrong? After all, it has been ten years since she last saw him."

"But what about the birthmark?" I asked.

"What if Sidney had a similar birthmark? How closely could Blanche have seen that birthmark, given the brief time she and Sidney were together?"

"But what about the fact that Not-Sid ran out on Sylvia Schuster right after being introduced to Blanche Becker?" I asked.

"Maybe he really did become ill."

"I don't buy it. All the evidence points to Not-Sid and Sheldon being the same person."

"All the *circumstantial* evidence," said Blake. "I'm not saying I don't agree with you, Gracie. I'm just saying that if Fox News couldn't confirm any of what Sylvia Schuster told the reporter, it might be why they didn't air the interview. And if Sylvia's interview is pulled, there's no reason to run any footage they filmed here tonight."

FIFTEEN

I spent a sleepless night tossing and turning in my mind, while forcing my body to lie still in order to keep from disturbing Blake. Beside me, my husband snored away, oblivious to my turmoil. Except for a restless wife, neither murder nor computer hackers nor reporters camped on our street nor the fear of living above an auto repair shop keeps my husband from his appointed Z's. Blake possesses the uncanny ability to turn off his brain for seven or eight hours each night. I wish I had such control over my own body.

I haven't had a decent night's sleep since Clinton was in the White House. If then. No matter what's going on in my life, my mind races at breakneck speed the moment my head hits the pillow. Right now, way too much was going on in my life and in my brain, even before Not-Sid's murder.

Some people count sheep; I lie awake listening to the voices in my head. Thea and Luke must be nocturnal characters because they insist on cavorting in my mind each night when I should be sleeping. If I wait until morning, I forget the scene that played out so vividly at three in the morning. So I often slip out of bed and head for the computer, thus depriving myself of even more sleep.

Tonight in order not to think about murder and computer hackers and reporters camped on our street and living above an auto repair shop, I pondered the blurb for my novel, going back to my original premise of a romantic comedy. Dealing with murder and mayhem in real life—not to mention being accused of taking part in such dastardly deeds—had soured me on the idea of writing romantic suspense or mystery.

I'd learned about the importance of the blurb at last month's Liberty States Fiction Writers meeting. A great blurb as part of a query letter will pique the interest of editors and agents, thus resulting in requests to read the author's manuscript.

By our next meeting I wanted a blurb that made editors and agents drool. However, unless I came up with something tonight, I'd miss my deadline. Honing the essence of Thea's and Luke's story down to two or three short paragraphs had proven anything but easy. Harder even than writing chapters. And I'd had little time to work on my blurb or anything else connected with my writing since discovering Not-Sid's dead body in the parking lot of the Moose Lodge last Wednesday evening.

Another fact I'd learned about blurbs was that it's best to memorize them. You never know when you'll stumble upon an editor or agent who will utter those most important five words, "Tell me about your book." So tonight in lieu of sleep and to the rhythmic snores of my husband, I formed blurb sentences in my head.

By two a.m. I'd constructed what I believed to be a drool-worthy blurb. I could only hope it sounded as brilliant five hours from now.

Hooking Mr. Right

After writing a doctoral thesis that exposed fraud in the pop-psychology genre, thirty-two year old professor Althea Chandler has to sacrifice her professional integrity to save her family from financial ruin. She secretly becomes bestselling romance guru Dr. Trulee Lovejoy, a self-proclaimed expert on how to catch a man, even though Thea is a miserable failure when it comes to relationships—especially those involving the opposite sex.

Burned by a failed marriage, Luke Bennett finds himself pursued by Dr. Lovejoy book-toting women after a gossip columnist dubs him New York's most eligible bachelor. When he at first mistakes Thea for one of the women out to snare him, sparks fly, but the two soon find themselves battling sparks of a less hostile nature, thanks in part to an alley cat named Cupid.

Luke believes he's finally found an honest woman. Unfortunately, Thea is anything but honest. She's got more secrets than the CIA and a desperate gossip columnist out to expose her. Cupid definitely has his work cut out for him.

~*~

I don't think I ever fell asleep. When Blake woke Saturday morning, he found me staring at the ceiling. At least I'd accomplished something during my sleepless night; I had my blurb. What I didn't have was enough energy to make it to my writers meeting.

After making a quick pit stop, Blake padded to the front of the house and peered out a window. "No reporters camped on our street," he reported.

The morning news mentioned nothing in any way, no matter how remotely, connected to me. One of the escaped prisoners was still on the loose and another crash victim, a serial rapist serving a life sentence without chance of parole, had succumbed to his injuries. No great loss there. Blanche Becker's arrest didn't even rate a five second sound bite.

"Here it is," said Blake.

He sat at the kitchen table, leafing through *The Star-Ledger* while I prepared a double batch of waffle batter, one batch for Connor, one for the rest of us to share. I didn't want my son starving between breakfast and lunch. "Here what is?"

"An article about Blanche Becker's arrest. Buried in the *Your Towns* section."

I leaned over his shoulder and stared at the headline, *Former Slum Baroness Charged with Masterminding Burglary Ring.*

Blake began to read aloud, "*Former real estate heiress Blanche Becker, was charged yesterday, along with her sons Samuel Craft Becker and Peter Remick Becker, in a burglary ring that targeted widows in Union and Somerset Counties.*

"*Becker's sons were apprehended after fleeing from a Bernards Township residence. During the arrest, police recovered several pieces of jewelry belonging to the homeowner.*"

"Hmm...sounds like Craft and Remick couldn't resist the temptation of helping themselves to a few things while searching for information on their father." I said.

"That's going to cost them," said Connor.

Blake continued reading. "*Their mother was later charged as a co-conspirator. Blanche Becker inherited a multi-million dollar real estate empire from her late father, Samuel Gottlieb, known back in the nineteen-sixties as The King of the Slum Lords in Newark and Irvington.*

"*Mrs. Becker is also the former wife of Sheldon Becker, who disappeared ten years ago, along with a purported twelve million dollars of his wife's family fortune, days prior to the couple being indicted on multiple counts of fraud and tax evasion. Sheldon Becker was declared dead seven years later. The missing money has never been recovered.*

"Mrs. Becker fell on hard times after her husband's disappearance when she was forced to liquidate much of her personal wealth to pay back taxes and settle the judgments levied against the couple.

"She and her sons were released after each posted bail of twenty-five thousand dollars."

"Not a word about Not-Sid's death," I said.

"Maybe the police are treating the two as separate cases," said Brooke. "At least for now, until they have proof that the two men were the same person."

I poured four cups of coffee and passed them around. "Tell me the truth," I asked Blake. "Do you believe Not-Sid was really Sheldon Becker?"

Blake folded the paper and exhaled a deep sigh. "I don't know, Gracie. The only evidence to indicate Sid was Sheldon is Blanche Becker's claim about that birthmark. I never noticed a birthmark behind Sidney Mandelbaum's ear—let alone one in the shape of Texas—did you?"

I splashed milk into my coffee and took a sip as I pondered his question. "No, but how often do you take note of the back of someone's head? Maybe if you're stuck in the slowest moving supermarket line ever or packed like sardines on a subway at rush hour, but other than that?"

"Which makes me wonder how Blanche would even have noticed the back of Sidney's head, especially if she were seated at the time they were introduced. Do you remember where Sylvia Schuster said she introduced them?"

"In the solarium."

"So it's likely Blanche was sitting at one of the card tables at the time."

"I suppose."

Blake stood. "Sit down. Sidney was about my height. Let's re-enact the most likely scenario."

When I took Blake's seat, he stood over me and extended his hand. "Nice to meet you, Mrs. Becker."

I shook his hand. "And you, Mr. Mandelbaum."

Blake turned to Brooke, playing the role of Sylvia Schuster. "My dear, would you excuse me for a moment? Nature calls." He pivoted and walked away, his back turned to me. At the doorway to the dining room Blake stopped and asked, "Where are your eyes, Gracie?"

"Staring at your back."

"Not at my head?"

"I'd have to crane my neck."

Blake spun around to face me. "Aha! Now do you believe Blanche recognized Sheldon's birthmark on Sidney?"

"Maybe she recognized his voice," said Connor.

Blake shook his head. "After ten years? Sidney sounded like every other seventy-something old geezer from New Jersey. There wasn't anything distinctive about his voice. No quirk. No lisp. No stutter. Nothing that would set him apart."

"What if it was a phrase he used?" asked Brooke.

"Or the way he tilted his head? Or some other gesture?" I added.

Blake shook his head. "According to what you overheard, Blanche said she recognized Sidney as Sheldon by the birthmark. Nothing more."

"Oh. Right." Darn his logic. So if Not-Sid wasn't Sheldon Becker, who was he? And why did someone kill him? "Why would Blanche think Not-Sid was Sheldon unless she recognized something about him?"

Blake shrugged. "Wishful thinking? For all we know, Blanche is suffering from dementia. Perhaps she saw what she wanted to see."

"And is now responsible for her sons committing a criminal act," I said.

"No one forced them to break into that townhouse," said Blake.

"Blanche coerced them."

"They're grown men, Gracie. They could have refused. And they certainly should have kept their sticky fingers off Suzette's jewelry."

I shrugged. "I guess it just proves that the Fig Newtons don't fall far from the tree. Anyway, I'm glad I didn't go into police work."

Blake shot me *The Look* but not for my Fig Newtons comment. "Aside from the obvious reasons, dare I ask?"

I sighed. "Not knowing the truth is so frustrating. It's a wonder the police ever solve any cases."

Another thought occurred to me as I poured batter onto the waffle iron. "If the police arrested Blanche, one or both of her sons must have ratted on her. Maybe one of them cut a deal for a lighter sentence."

"Or Detective Menendez used what you overheard to squeeze a confession out of one of them."

"Neither seemed too happy about having to do their mother's dirty work."

"Yet greedy enough to do it in the end."

"If Blanche is full of crap about Not-Sid being Sheldon, where does that leave the murder investigation?" I asked.

"In the hands of the police, where it belongs, Gracie. Remember your promise to me."

"I haven't forgotten. I'm just curious as to how they'll go about solving the murder of a man with a fake identity. If they don't know who Not-Sid really was or where he was living, how can they possibly find his killer?"

"Not every crime is solved," said Blake.

"Which means someone will get away with murder if this one isn't, said Brooke."

Blake shrugged. "Happens every day."

"But this murder is different," I said.

"How so?" asked Connor.

"Your father and I knew the victim."

"We knew a man who didn't exist," said Blake.

Another thought occurred to me as I served the waffles. "What if Not-Sid was the killer's target, not whoever Not-Sid really was?"

Blake wrinkled his forehead. I think it took him a moment to puzzle out what I'd said, even though it made perfect sense to me. You'd think after all these years together, Blake would understand Gracie Speak.

"Sweetheart, Sidney Mandelbaum took on a stolen identity because he was hiding from someone or something."

"You know that for a fact?"

"Of course not, but it's the only logical explanation for changing one's identity. It stands to reason that whatever he had run from finally caught up with him. For all we know, he was in Witness Protection."

"That's one theory," I said.

"You have another?"

"Not-Sid either swindled or tried to swindle several of the women he met through Relatively Speaking."

Blake chuckled. "You think one of those little old ladies killed him?"

"Of course not. But maybe he swindled other people we don't know about. People who were capable of killing him. He took on the real Sidney Mandelbaum's identity about three months ago. What's to say he didn't have another fake identity prior to that?"

Blake's forehead unwrinkled. He nodded. "I suppose that's possible."

"For all we know, he may have had a string of fake identities, going back years. And maybe an equal number of plastic surgeries to go along with each new identity."

"Ouch," said Brooke. "Talk about sacrificing for your career."

"One thing you're all forgetting," said Connor.

"What's that?" I asked.

"Eventually, the police will be able to determine if your Not-Sid was really Sheldon Becker. All they have to do is compare his DNA to that of Blanche Becker's sons."

Blake patted Connor on the back. "And that's why my boy got into Columbia." Then he turned to me. "And why you and I are leaving the rest of the investigation to the police."

SIXTEEN

"I mean it," said Blake. "We've had enough excitement the last few days for several lifetimes."

"Fine with me," I said. "Besides, we've hit the proverbial brick wall in our investigation of Not-Sid and the questioning of his dates. I have no clue where to find more clues."

"Nowhere. We're out of the sleuthing business, Gracie. Leave it to the police. We're spending a relaxing weekend at home, and come Monday, our lives are returning to normal."

I wanted to ask if Blake's definition of normal meant pre-Relatively Speaking normal, but I thought better of bringing up my business at the moment. Besides, I had a sinking feeling Relatively Speaking would fizzle out on its own. Bad publicity would kill my little enterprise once the press found themselves with another slow news day and began sniffing around the circumstances surrounding Not-Sid's death and Sheldon's disappearance.

"We have plans this evening," I reminded him.

"What plans?"

"Reinhold's community theater."

Blake slapped his forehead. "I forgot."

"We have to go."

He grimaced. "I know."

Tom Reinhold, the head of Blake's department, had convinced the university to support a local community theater he ran. I often wondered if blackmail was somehow involved because the guy lacked any discernable talent. However, that didn't keep him from not only directing each season's offerings but casting himself in every male lead, no matter the age disparity.

As painful as it was to sit through Hamlet's soliloquy spoken by a senior citizen with a Jersey accent, Blake not only felt obligated to purchase tickets for every show, university politics deemed it necessary for us to make an appearance on each opening night.

"What play will he be butchering this evening?" asked Blake.

I checked the tickets hanging on the refrigerator door. "*Follies.*"

Blake groaned. "A musical? We have to listen to him sing? His acting is bad enough."

"We don't have to go, do we?" asked Brooke. "I have plans tonight."

"I'll make some," said Connor.

"You're both off the hook," said Blake. "Now that you're in college, I can get away with buying only two tickets."

In the past Blake had been pressured to purchase four tickets for each show. Reinhold insisted that teenagers these days weren't exposed to nearly enough culture. Not wanting to get stuck with a killer teaching schedule any given semester, my husband never told the man his acting was the antithesis of culture. Neither did the rest of the department faculty and staff—or their spouses. Four times a year we all suffered together in silence for two to three hours.

~*~

Follies, a tale of aging showgirls who come together one last time for a cast reunion, features a large company of older performers. Given past Reinhold productions, we were in for a long evening of amateurs butchering Sondheim.

We settled into our seats and made small talk with Greg Jordan, one of Blake's colleagues, and his wife Shelly. As soon as the lights began to dim and the small orchestra struck the first notes of the overture, Blake leaned back, closed his eyes, and said, "Wake me when it's over."

"Don't snore," I warned him.

As the overture ended and the curtain rose, an overweight older man in an ill-fitting tuxedo lumbered across the stage and began singing a slightly off-key rendition of "Beautiful Girls." While he belted out the lyrics, the showgirls entered from either side of the wings and took their places at the front of the stage. I was about to close my own eyes when one of the women caught my attention. Then another. And another. And finally a fourth. I nudged Blake with my elbow and whispered into his ear, "Open your eyes!"

He whispered back, "Not until it's over. Listening is bad enough."

"Really, Blake, you have to see this."

"See what?"

"Any of those actresses look familiar to you?"

Blake squinted at the stage. "The woman in the pink sequins.

Isn't that—?"

"Maureen Boland. Keep looking. That's Mary Louise Franklin two women to her left, Leila Raffelino on her right, and Suzette Stephanovich standing next to Leila."

"Highly coincidental," said Blake.

"If you believe in coincidence." Although coincidences do happen, what were the odds of four of Not-Sid's dates knowing each other?

Blake and I definitely needed to duck out of the theater before the cast members joined the attendees at the opening night reception. I couldn't run the risk of Maureen Boland accosting me about her missing stock certificates, not with my husband's colleagues within earshot.

"I feel a migraine coming on," I whispered to Blake.

"A perfect excuse for leaving," he said. "Try to look green."

At intermission I accessed what limited acting skills I possessed—which certainly weren't any worse than those showcased onstage. Greg and Shelley saw right through me. "Wish I'd thought of that," said Greg.

"No, really. I'm in terrible pain."

"Aren't we all," said Shelly. She patted my arm and winked at me. "I'm sure you'll feel much better once you're home."

They promised to offer our congratulations to Tom Reinhold and regrets that we couldn't stay for the party. "But only if I get dibs on the migraine for the next production," said Shelly.

"Absolutely," I said.

"So what do you think?" I asked Blake as we drove home.

"About your migraine? You need to work on your queasy look."

"About Maureen, Mary Louise, Leila, and Suzette knowing

each other. Maybe one of them had something to do with Not-Sid's death."

"Hell hath no fury like a woman scorned, but do you really think any one of those women is capable of sneaking up behind Sidney and bashing his skull?"

"Maureen is big enough."

"Maureen is all flab, no muscle. Sidney could bench press her. Besides, with all that jangling bling, he'd hear her coming a mile away. She'd never get the drop on him."

"Maybe she wasn't wearing any jewelry that night. Besides, dead men can't bench press."

Blake gave me *The Look*. "When he was alive, Gracie."

I knew that.

I also knew that Not-Sid had scammed Maureen Boland but he'd treated Mary Louise Franklin like—in her words—an empress, sparing no expense in the wining-and-dining department. How had his dates with Leila Raffelino and Suzette Stephanovich gone? Leila had refused to speak with us and Suzette wasn't home when we showed up at her townhouse. Were either of them scammed? Dropped after one date? Or as with Mary Louise, had their wealth caused Not-Sid to look beyond a short scam? Was he stringing each woman along until he had a handle on the size of their portfolios before popping the question to one of them?

"We need to speak with Leila and Suzette," I said.

Blake speared me with *The Look*. "*We* are doing no such thing. You promised to leave the investigating to the professionals, remember?"

"I know but—"

"But nothing. You can call Detective Menendez to tell her

what we saw this evening. Nothing more."

"I'll call her Monday."

"What's wrong with tomorrow? Or even right now?"

"What's the rush? Let Menendez enjoy her weekend. None of those women saw us. It's not like they're all going to flee the country this evening."

~*~

Detective Menendez didn't answer her phone when I called her first thing Monday morning. I left a message, asking her to call me back. Shortly after hanging up, I was surprised to receive a phone call from Leila Raffelino.

"I'm so sorry I wasn't able to see you the other day," she said. "Can I assume you want to speak with me about poor, dear Sidney?"

Poor, dear Sidney? Leila didn't sound like the victim of a Not-Sid scam attempt. Given where she lived, I mentally moved her into the same column as Mary Louise. "Yes, I do."

"I have appointments later today. Why don't you come over now?"

Blake was teaching this morning, but I didn't want to pass up the opportunity to meet with Leila. "I'm on my way."

Fifteen minutes later I stood in the lobby of Leila's complex and gave my name to the guard. After a brief phone call to Leila, he directed me toward the elevator. "Apartment 4G," he said.

Leila was waiting for me at her open door. "Do come in, dear. I've made coffee."

Leila Raffelino had the requisite casabas, plus the booty to match. She showcased both with a Spandex wardrobe far more fitting for someone a quarter of her age. Her jet black hair came out of a bottle, and she applied makeup with a trowel over a face that had already gone under the knife at least one too many times. She obviously wasn't going gently into that good night of old age. I'm certain she thought she looked gorgeous; I thought she looked freakish.

She led me into an immaculate living room tiled in marble and decorated in high-end Rococo furnishings, extremely ornate and covered in gold leaf. A plush oriental carpet covered most of the living room floor. I took a seat on a red damask couch. Leila sat across from me on a matching chair, a marble and gilt coffee table between us. "Cream and sugar?" she asked, pouring from a silver coffee urn into a delicate porcelain floral teacup rimmed in gold.

"Just cream, please."

She added a splash of cream and passed me the cup. "I was so sorry to hear about Sidney," she said. "And to go in such a horrible way! I hope he didn't suffer long."

Chances were, Not-Sid never knew what hit him, then stabbed him in the heart. But I didn't voice my thoughts. Instead, I took a sip of my coffee before asking, "How did you find out about his murder?"

"A detective came to question me. So what can I do for you Mrs. Elliott?"

"I'm distraught over Sidney's murder. My husband and I were with him when it happened."

Leila's thin, penciled eyebrows shot up. "You saw the killer?"

"No, Sidney had stepped outside for a cigar. When he didn't return within a reasonable amount of time, we went in search of him. He was already dead when we found him."

"How shocking!"

"Frightening, actually. We had no idea if the killer was still nearby." I took another sip of coffee. "Anyway, I know the police can be intimidating. I thought if I spoke with you, you might remember something Sidney may have said at some point that could help find his killer."

"Like what?"

I shrugged. "I don't know. Perhaps someone or something he mentioned in passing that may not have seemed important at the time?"

Leila stared at me; an odd expression settled over her face. Make that *faces*. Two Leila's sat in front of me, then four, all spinning around the room, along with the furniture, to the rhythm of my teacup clattering against the saucer.

SEVENTEEN

I couldn't move, not even my mouth. My head pounded. I struggled to open my eyes and found myself still in Leila Raffelino's living room. Only instead of being seated on her couch, I was tied to one of her Rococo dining room chairs, my arms bound behind me, my legs secured to each of the chair's front legs. A gag was wrapped tightly around my mouth.

Leila was nowhere in sight, but I heard voices coming from another part of the apartment, voices I recognized.

"What do we do with her?" asked Mary Louise Franklin.

"We have to get rid of her," said Leila.

"Permanently?"

"Absolutely," said Maureen Boland. "She's snooping around too much. We can't risk her figuring out what happened."

"What happened never should have happened." I couldn't pinpoint that voice, but it had to belong to Suzette Stephanovich. "You screwed up, Leila, and now we're all in trouble."

"It's not my fault!"

"How is it not your fault?" asked Mary Louise. "You're the one with the family connections. You hired the guy."

Family connections? As in family or *family*? Were they talking Mafia?

"No, I hired the guy who hired the guy."

"Why didn't your guy do it himself?" asked Maureen.

"Because you didn't want to pay what he charges. If you all want to blame someone, blame Maureen for being so cheap."

"That still doesn't explain why he killed Sidney," said Mary Louise. "You must have said something to lead him to believe you wanted Sidney dead."

"Absolutely," said Suzette. "Otherwise he'd still be alive, and we wouldn't be in this pickle."

"I didn't."

"What did you say?" asked Maureen. "Exactly."

"I don't remember. Something about how he tried to con us, and we wanted to teach him a lesson."

"So you didn't tell him *not* to kill Sidney?" asked Suzette.

"I didn't tell him we wanted Sidney dead, but you can't expect me to remember the conversation verbatim!"

"Why not?" asked Mary Louise. "You remember your lines on stage, don't you?"

"That's different. I study my lines for a play. I don't memorize conversations I have with people."

"This wasn't just any conversation," said Maureen.

"Maybe Sidney recognized him, and they struggled," said Leila.

"You're grasping at straws," said Mary Louise. "It's clear now how this happened. It's all your fault, Leila."

"And now you've made matters that much worse," said Suzette. "Why is that woman even here? I thought you refused to see her the other day."

"I did, but then I got to thinking, what if she knows more than she's letting on? We couldn't take that chance."

"You should have consulted us first," said Mary Louise.

"Especially since you did more than just talk to her," said Maureen. "Why did you drug her? That wasn't in the script."

"I decided it was best to tie up loose ends. So I improvised."

"No one asked you to improvise!" said Maureen. "You shouldn't have called her in the first place. But since you were so concerned about what she knew, you should have just answered her questions and let her leave. No one suspected us. Not the police, not her."

"You don't know that," said Leila. "She could have been playing us just like Sidney did. Only instead of trying to scam us, she was trying to pin a murder on us."

"There was no indication of that," said Suzette. "We all played our parts. Everything was working out fine until you *improvised*. Now look what you've done!"

"You never were any good at improvisation," said Maureen. "Then again, you never were very good at acting, either."

"How dare you!"

"Enough!" said Suzette. "We're now going to have two dead bodies on our hands, and we can't have hers tied to us in any way. Not unless you all want to live out the rest of your lives behind bars."

"Killing her will look awfully coincidental," said Maureen. "The police are bound to get suspicious."

"Not if her death looks like an accident," said Leila.

"How are we going to do that?" asked Mary Louise. "And what about getting her out of the apartment? The guard saw her come in. Not to mention the security cameras all over this place."

"I'll make a call," said Leila.

"Like you did last time?" asked Suzette. "That worked out so well."

"I'll make sure he does it himself this time. He can do anything for a price."

"We've already paid twenty grand," said Maureen. "How much more is this going to cost us?"

"I don't know," said Leila. "I'm not his accountant."

"I don't think we have any other choice," said Suzette. "Not after what's happened today. Make the call."

I listened as Leila explained the situation to someone on the other end of the phone. When she hung up, she told the others, "He said he can do it, but he wants forty."

"Forty!" shrieked Maureen. "Are you kidding me?"

"You get what you pay for," said Leila.

"You should pay for this yourself," said Maureen. "Your *improvising* is costing us all another ten grand."

"Fine," said Leila. "And while I'm at it, I'll pay to have him get rid of you."

"Stop it!" said Suzette. "We're all in this together."

"One more thing," said Leila. "He won't be able to arrive for at least an hour. Maybe two. He's in the middle of something."

"Will she stay unconscious that long?" asked Suzette.

"She should be out for hours," said Leila. "I gave her a double dose."

I had no idea what she'd drugged me with, but it was probably a good thing I'd only had a few sips of the coffee. The clock on her mantle told me I'd been out for less than an hour, and with each passing minute the pain receded, and I felt more clearheaded.

"What do we do until he gets here?" asked Mary Louise.

"We can watch television," said Leila. "My favorite soap is on in a few minutes."

I heard the television turn on. The women continued talking, but their conversation competed with the noise of the television, and I could no longer make out what they said. I'd heard enough, anyway. Somehow I had to get out of that apartment before a hired killer came to drag me away.

I began squirming, trying to loosen my restraints without making any noise that might raise the suspicions of the women in the other room. They'd bound me with what felt like yarn. I couldn't see to be sure. I suppose Leila didn't have any rope or duct tape, and for that I sent up a thank-you to the heavens. If I continued to rub the yarn against the edge of the wood on the back of the chair, it should eventually fray enough to break easily.

As I worked, I thought about what I'd heard. At some point the four women must have realized they were all dating the same man. Once they began comparing notes, they figured out his con game and decided to teach him a lesson. But something had gone terribly wrong, and Not-Sid wound up dead. They then concocted intricate stories to cover their butts.

I felt the yarn start to give way and tugged, but just as I was about to free myself, I heard the distinctive clickity-clack of stilettos on a marble floor. I closed my eyes and slumped my head onto my chest.

"She's still out cold," Leila yelled. A moment later I heard the sound of dishes rattling around in the kitchen. I waited until she returned to the room with the television, then slipped my wrists from the yarn and began to untie my feet. Once free, I grabbed my purse and tiptoed out of the apartment.

The adrenaline rush that had carried me from the building to my car disappeared once I unlocked the driver's side door, slid behind the wheel, and beeped the locks. I couldn't even insert the key into the ignition. My limbs shook too violently. I began to hyperventilate and cry at the same time.

I don't have time for this! I double-fisted the steering wheel, closed my eyes, and forced myself to take slow, deep breaths while I counted each inhale and exhale. At the twentieth repetition I'd calmed down enough to place a call to Detective Menendez. Once again, I got her voice mail.

This time I left a more detailed message. *Stay calm*, I told myself, hoping my voice remained steady enough for my message to make sense. "Detective, this is Grace Elliott. I know who killed Sidney Mandelbaum." I proceeded to tell her about my visit to Leila Raffelino, how she'd drugged me, and how I overheard her and the other three women planning my murder. "As soon as that soap opera is over, they're going to realize I've escaped. Call me!"

I disconnected the call, threw the car into DRIVE and hightailed it out of the Dakota West visitors' parking lot.

In the story of my life, I became the TSTL—the too stupid to live heroine. Any decent writer knows not to write a TSTL. I'd *never* write a TSTL. Why had I acted like one? Because it never occurred to me that four little old ladies could be cold-hearted killers.

I think I held my breath until I arrived home. I was never so happy to see Blake's car parked in the driveway. I parked my car next to his, raced into the house, and ran into his arms.

"Gracie, what's wrong?"

"Just hold me." I started crying huge blubbering sobs as I held onto my husband for dear life.

"Gracie, you're scaring me. What happened?"

I shook my head, unable to speak. Blake walked us both over to the sofa in the family room and sat us down. "Shh." He rocked me in his arms, rubbing one hand up and down my back the way he used to calm Connor and Brooke when nightmares woke them. His other hand held my head against his shoulder as he whispered soothing words into my ear.

I don't know how long we sat like that. Eventually, I ran out of both steam and tears and began hiccupping. "Can I let go to get you some water?" he asked.

I nodded. Blake released me, returning shortly with a glass of water. I sipped slowly.

"Were you in an accident?" He sat down beside me and held my free hand in both of his.

I shook my head.

"Are you hurt?"

I took a deep breath before I spoke. "It's complicated."

"Take your time."

"Promise you won't kill me."

To his credit, Blake didn't start yelling at me. He didn't even give me *The Look*. I think I'd scared him too much. He simply nodded and said, "I promise."

Once the hiccups subsided, I began. Slowly. Haltingly. Explaining Leila's call. "She sounded upset about Not-Sid's death. She invited me over."

"And?"

I took a deep breath. I couldn't meet my husband's eyes. Instead, I stared at my lap and mumbled, "She drugged me."

"What!" Blake sprang to his feet, yanking me with him. "I'm taking you to the hospital."

My eyes welled back up with tears. "Please sit down."

"Gracie, you need to be checked out."

"Later."

Blake released me. I fell back onto the sofa. He perched on the edge of the cushion, his body angled toward me. "Go on."

I related the rest of the events to him. "I don't think Leila realized I'd only taken a few sips of coffee before I passed out. That's why I woke up so soon."

"You're lucky she didn't kill you. Did you hear her mention what she used to doctor the coffee?"

"No, just that she gave me a double dose."

Blake stood again. "Now we're going to the hospital, Gracie."

I didn't argue with him. The hospital seemed a far safer place than staying at home waiting for a killer to show up.

~*~

Three hours later—most of the time spent cooling our heels, first in the emergency waiting room, then in an examining room—a doctor pronounced me healthy. Whatever Leila had used to lace my coffee hadn't done any permanent damage.

Detective Menendez marched into the examining room as soon as the doctor left. She must have been waiting in the hall. "What part of keep your nose out of my investigation didn't you understand, Mrs. Elliott?"

I blurted out the first lame excuse that came to mind. "She called me! Besides, you didn't answer your phone this morning."

"So because I was testifying in a court case, you decided to play Miss Marple again?"

"I think my wife has finally learned her lesson," said Blake.

Menendez glared at me. "I certainly hope so."

"I have. Cross my heart." I emphasized my words by drawing a cross with my index finger over my hospital gown.

"And hope to die?"

Which had almost happened. I shuddered. "That, too."

She nodded. "When you're up to it, I'll need you to come in to give a statement."

"What about Leila, Mary Louise, Suzette, and Maureen?"

"Behind bars for now."

"And the guy they hired to kill me?"

"We haven't been able to determine who he is. Raffelino lawyered up. She's not talking."

EIGHTEEN

"So I've got some Mafia hit man after me?" I started hyperventilating.

Blake wrapped his arm around my shoulders to keep me from tumbling off the examination table. "Steady, sweetheart. Take slow, deep breaths."

I shuddered through each one. Eventually my breathing normalized, but my anxiety level remained high. How had everything gone so terribly wrong? All I'd wanted to do was earn enough money to keep us from being forced to move to an apartment above an auto repair shop in Newark.

Well, I certainly didn't have to worry about that anymore. Pretty soon I'd be sleeping with the fishes, and Blake could live comfortably on the proceeds from my life insurance policy. Unless the hit man targeted him, too. At that thought I began hyperventilating again.

Menendez pulled a deep frown; her eyebrows knit together. "No one mentioned anything about the Mafia, Mrs. Elliott."

I squeezed Blake's hand and forced out a few more shaky calming breaths, mentally counting as I slowly inhaled and exhaled before I spoke. "Mary Louise said Leila has family connections. That's how they got someone to take care of Not-Sid. You and I both know in New Jersey *family connections* can only mean one thing."

"You watch too much TV, Mrs. Elliott."

"Do I? If that weren't the case, Leila would cut a deal for a get-out-of-jail-free card."

When Menendez made no attempt to refute my statement, my panic grew exponentially. Tears cascaded down my cheeks. I buried my face in my hands and wailed, "Oh God! I don't want to die."

"We're going to keep you safe while we hunt down this guy," she said.

"How?" asked Blake.

"I'm assigning a detail to protect your wife."

Why did that do absolutely nothing to quell my fear? Because every violent TV and movie scene I'd ever watched now bombarded my brain. If I survived this hit man, I was switching my entertainment viewing to nothing but giant yellow birds and purple dinosaurs. Maybe the occasional romcom. And I was definitely giving up on the idea of writing mystery or romantic suspense. Living the real deal was enough to scare me straight back into the loving arms of the romance genre.

~*~

Two policemen camped out in a squad car in front of our house the remainder of the day, replaced by another team overnight. I couldn't sleep, but I pretended to. Beside me, Blake did likewise. Since nothing ever keeps my husband from his Z's, I knew he had to be scared out of his mind. I'm sure he knew I was awake just as I knew he was, but we didn't speak. Voicing our fears would only make them more real.

Throughout the night my mind raced with all sorts of scenarios involving a hit man silently breaking in through a window at the back of the house and murdering me in my bed. How would cops sitting in front of the house know what was going on at the back of the house?

Or he might break into a neighbor's house and target me with a high-powered sniper rifle. To thwart such an attempt I decided to keep all the blinds drawn at all times. I didn't think a hit man would be stupid enough to spray our house with bullets, hoping to hit his target.

But what if he planted a bomb? Or tossed a Molotov cocktail through a window? Or...or...or....The possibilities were endless, and I was driving myself crazy by silently dwelling on them.

I expected to feel like a zombie the next morning, but fear and anxiety acted like an intravenous caffeine drip. By seven a.m. I'd also downed three cups of coffee.

I was about to pour a fourth cup when Blake stopped me. "You're wired enough, Gracie. I don't want to find you bouncing off the walls when I get home."

"Bouncing is good. It means I'll still be alive."

Blake sighed. "I really don't want to leave you alone today."

"I know, but you have to." Tuesdays were Blake's longest day of teaching. "Besides, you can't blow off a meeting you scheduled with the dean weeks ago."

"He'd understand."

"That would require too much explanation. I don't want the entire university knowing what's going on, do you?"

He sighed again. "Look who's being the logical one now."

"You should be glad some of your left-brained logic has finally rubbed off on me after all these years." Too bad it had taken a hit man to bring me to my senses. I was officially swearing off all right-brained/harebrained ideas for the remainder of my life—assuming I survived long enough to have a remainder of my life.

At eight o'clock Blake reluctantly headed off to campus. Since the police had returned our computers after Tiffany's arrest, I tried to work on my novel. However, I spent the next three hours staring at a blinking cursor—when I wasn't jumping out of my skin every time a car drove down the street or someone in the neighborhood powered up a leaf blower. It's damned hard to be creative when you're worrying if you'll live long enough to see your work in print.

I thought about getting together with Natalie and Myra, but quickly decided against the idea. I wouldn't put my friends in harm's way and risk them becoming collateral damage.

My lack of sleep finally caught up with me by noon. All the adrenaline and caffeine could no longer keep Mr. Sandman at bay. And that blinking cursor had acted like a hypnotist's swaying pocket watch. I gave in and curled up on my bed.

When I jolted awake sometime later, I didn't know what shocked me more—that someone had a hand over my mouth and a gun pointed at my head or the identity of that someone.

NINETEEN

Rudy Klingerhoff leaned closer, his lips brushing my ear. In a menacing growl he whispered, "Scream and I shoot you right here. Understand?"

I nodded.

He withdrew his hand from my mouth. "Why?" I mouthed, unable to force any sound from my vocal chords.

"Don't take it personally."

With that, my anger flared. I found my voice, but it came out as a croak. "How am I supposed to take it, Rudy?"

He shrugged. "It's business."

"You're the hit man Leila hired."

"Small world, isn't it?"

"You don't have to do this. The police already have Leila in custody. She'll rat you out eventually."

"She knows better than to do that."

"I'll pay you double what she promised you." I'd definitely wind up living above that auto repair shop in Newark, but at least

I'd be alive.

"Sorry. That wouldn't be ethical. I gave my word."

"An ethical hit man? Isn't that an oxymoron?"

"I'm not here to debate philosophy with you. Get up." He yanked my arm, nearly dislocating my shoulder as he pulled me to a seated position. A lifetime of bowling had given Rudy the upper-body strength of the average gym rat half his age.

"There are cops parked outside."

"Not anymore. A few minutes ago they received a credible tip that the guy holding the contract on you is holed up in a house in East Orange. By the time they realize they were sent on a wild goose chase, you and I will be long gone." He dragged me to my feet. "Put your shoes on."

I slipped into the ballerina-style Keens I'd been wearing before my nap. "I have to use the bathroom," I said.

Rudy smirked. "Nice try."

"No, really. I suffer from stress-induced plumbing problems." And boy, was I ever stressed.

Rudy dragged me toward the master bathroom and poked his head in. "You can go, but I'm leaving the door open to keep an eye on you."

"I never took you for a pervert, Rudy."

"I'm not. I don't want any funny business."

"You're the one with the gun. What can I do?"

He released his grip on my arm and waved me into the bathroom. A four-foot high tiled pony wall topped with frosted glass running to the ceiling separated the toilet from the soaking tub. Standing in the entrance of the bathroom, Rudy would only see a blurry image of my head as I sat on the toilet. And that's exactly what I was counting on.

Long ago I'd gotten into the habit of carrying my cell phone in a pocket because I never had enough time to dig it out of my purse before the caller hung up. My one pre-requisite for all new clothing purchases was that the pants, skirt, or dress have a pocket for my phone. I've passed up buying many outfits for lack of a suitable phone pocket. I was counting on Rudy expecting that, like most women, I carried my phone in my purse.

As I sat on the toilet, I slipped the phone from my right front jeans pocket, flipped the side switch to silent, dialed 911, then placed the phone back into the pocket. Even though Rudy never took his eyes off me, he remained clueless.

All I needed to do now was get him to talk—and hope the dispatcher on the other end would hear us through the denim fabric. "Where are you taking me?" I asked as I flushed the toilet and headed to the sink.

He grabbed my arm and pulled me from the bathroom without allowing me to wash my hands. "What difference does it make? You're not going to live to tell anyone."

As he dragged me down the stairs, I asked, "Isn't there anything I can do to keep you from killing me, Rudy?"

"None. I'm a man of my word."

"I had no idea hit men had such scruples."

"Of course we have scruples. I'm no serial killer."

"Aren't you?"

"Of course, not. I don't do this for fun. It's my profession. I only kill when I'm hired to do a job. Like a soldier."

"And that makes it okay? It doesn't bother you that you're taking an innocent life?"

"It's a job. One I'm good at. So don't get any ideas thinking you're going to play on my sympathies. I've heard every excuse in the book over the years."

With one arm wrapped around my waist and his other hand poking the gun into my ribs, Rudy led me out the back door and across my driveway into my next-door neighbor's back yard. We then cut through to the street parallel to my street.

We continued halfway down the block to a black Nissan Pathfinder with dark tinted windows. Rudy beeped open the driver side door and shoved me across, over the console, into the passenger seat. "Buckle up," he said.

I couldn't help but laugh at the irony. "Really? Why do you care? You're going to kill me anyway."

With a perfectly straight face he said, "It's against the law not to wear a seatbelt."

"Murder is against the law, too, in case you haven't heard."

He reached over and grabbed the seatbelt, stretching it across my torso. "And I don't want you getting any funny ideas," he said, clicking the fastener in place, "like trying to leap from the car."

"Wouldn't think of it, Rudy. I can't outrun a bullet."

"Good girl." He squeezed my thigh. My mind immediately flashed back to the dirty old man who'd set my demise in motion. If I hadn't been swayed by Mandelbaum Moolah, I wouldn't now be on my way to my own funeral.

"However," he continued, "I don't take chances."

He grabbed my left wrist and slapped one end of a handcuff on it. Then he reached across my body again, looped the other part through the grab bar, and cuffed my right wrist. "Not comfortable, Rudy."

"Not meant to be."

Rudy was a sociopath masquerading as Cary Grant, a perfect cover. Who would ever suspect sweet Rudy Klingerhoff, the good-looking, good-natured king of New Jersey bowling was a coldblooded gun-for-hire?

He switched on the ignition and pulled away from the curb, the gun resting in his lap. We drove in silence for a few minutes, Rudy maintaining the speed limit, as we traveled through the streets of Westfield.

I needed to get him talking again. From everything I knew about 911 calls, someone should be on the other end of the line listening to our conversation. They'd track the GPS in my phone, but I had no clue as to how quickly such technology actually worked. From writing workshops I'd attended, I knew never to use television shows as research for my books. TV time had no correlation to real-life time. What actors accomplished in an hour took real cops days, weeks, or even months. I needed to give the police more clues to our location and destination.

Of course, most of what I knew about 911 also came from watching movies and TV shows. My life now depended on the slim chance that all those fictional stories were based on factual technology and actual police procedures and that the dispatcher hadn't hung up when no one responded to her initial inquiry.

Still, a slim chance beat no chance. So I started talking again, trying my hardest to drop clues into my end of the conversation without letting on that the police might be listening. "I thought your kids took away your car keys, Rudy. Where'd you get the black Pathfinder?"

He laughed. "They don't know about this car."

"Do they know what you do for a living?"

He shot me a withering look. "They think I'm a retired long-haul trucker."

"Were you?"

"Never. Been in this business since leaving the army in seventy-two."

Which meant Rudy had spent over four decades murdering people for a living. Even if I didn't survive, at least the police would have a taped confession to lock him up for the rest of his life. I'd be Rudy's last kill, sparing countless future victims, although not exactly the legacy I'd envisioned for myself.

Rudy pulled onto the Garden State Parkway and picked up speed as we headed east but quickly slowed when we hit backed-up traffic shortly past the Kenilworth exit. "Looks like an accident up ahead," I said. "Probably all the way past the Union tolls. Maybe as far as Montclair. You know the Parkway. One minor fender-bender can tie up traffic for hours."

He turned and glared at me. "What are you, a goddamn traffic report?"

I changed the subject. "You have no regrets?" I asked.

"About what?"

"All the people you've killed. It doesn't bother you?"

He shook his head. "Like I said, it's a job. Paid the bills. Put food on the table. Clothed my wife and kids. A job is a job."

"That's the way you think of it? Like selling used cars? Or life insurance?"

He shrugged. "This pays better. The army teaches you to compartmentalize."

I couldn't prevent the shudder that coursed through my body. Tears filled my eyes. I'd never met a man with so little regard for human life—mine and the countless others he'd abruptly ended over the years. "Not even one person you regret killing?"

"None. Most of them needed killing."

"I don't."

"You do to someone."

I drew in a shaky breath. "Are you going to make me suffer, Rudy?"

He looked surprised. "Hell no. I'm not a sadist, Mrs. Elliott. Besides, I like you. I'll make it quick. You'll never know what hit you."

I took little comfort in that. Had he planned to drag out my death, the cops would have more time to find me. "Will you leave my body somewhere for the cops to find?"

"Why would I do that?"

"So my family can bury me."

He shook his head. "Sorry. Can't leave any evidence behind."

The tears that had welled up behind my eyes coursed down my cheeks. "They'll never know what happened to me."

He shrugged. "No point in crying. Them's the breaks."

I should have made a grab for his gun before Rudy cuffed me. But what if he'd wrestled it out of my hand before I had a chance to shoot? Or I couldn't squeeze the trigger? I'd never shot a gun before, never even held one. If it had a safety, I wouldn't know how to unlock it. Not that any of this conjecturing now mattered. I was in no position to do anything except pray the police found me before Rudy carried out his hit.

At the Union tolls he exited onto Rt. 78, quickly turning onto the first exit ramp into Newark. He drove for a few blocks before turning into a driveway. "Is this where you're going to kill me, Rudy? A house on Keer Avenue in Newark?"

"Maybe."

He stopped in front of a one-car garage at the back of the property, set the parking brake and hopped out of the car, leaving the engine running. The garage had double doors secured with a bulky metal chain and heavy-duty padlock. Rudy pulled a key from his pocked, unlocked the lock, slipped the chain from one door handle, and swung the doors open. Then he returned to the car and pulled into the garage. "Make yourself comfortable," he said after parking the car.

Panic flooded through me. "You're leaving me here? In this garage?"

He opened his door and stepped out of the car. "Only until I have confirmation of payment."

"Leila's in police custody. How do you expect her to pay you?"

"She'll get out on bail. Eventually."

"Rudy, please!" I started crying again, begging. "Don't lock me up in here. I'm claustrophobic." I wasn't, but I was quickly running out of options. What if he dropped dead from a heart attack or stroke in the next few minutes? How long before someone found me? "Can't I wait in the house with you?" I pleaded.

"Sorry. Too risky. You stay here 'til the money is transferred into my off-shore account. Then I'll put you out of your misery." He slammed the door but opened it immediately and stuck his head back in. "One more thing," he added. "If you start screaming, I'll shove a ball gag in your mouth. Trust me. You don't want me to do that. So be a good girl, and keep quiet."

He slammed the door again, this time beeping the doors locked. A moment later the garage door swung shut, engulfing me in darkness. I heard him pull the heavy chain back through the door handles, trapping me inside.

I gulped back my tears and fought to force out words, speaking loudly but not shouting. I needed to make sure I could be heard through the denim covering my phone but not loud enough that

Rudy might hear me. For all I knew, he was lurking on the other side of the garage wall.

"I sure hope someone is listening because I'm in deep shit here. This is Gracie Elliott. Rudy Klingerhoff is the hit man hired by Leila Raffelino. He kidnapped me and locked me in the garage of a house on the second block of Keer Avenue in Newark. A white and brick house with a red door. I'd really appreciate a rescue. Sooner rather than later would be ideal. I'm strapped in and handcuffed awkwardly to the grab bar. I can't move, and I'm losing circulation in my hands and arms. My muscles are on fire.

"And one more thing, just in case you didn't hear us earlier—if you let Leila Raffelino out on bail, I'm a goner because Rudy intends to kill me as soon as he receives payment for the hit."

I thought about what I must be putting Blake through. He'd come home to find the cops gone from the front of the house. Me missing, my car still in the driveway, my purse on the kitchen counter. He'd immediately figure out the hit man had me.

Why hadn't I listened to him when he first told me Relatively Speaking was a bad idea? Blake's words to me after we were arrested in front of Suzette's townhouse in Bernards Township haunted me. *I want us to live to a ripe old age together, rocking on the front porch, enjoying grandchildren, griping about our aches and pains. I don't want a future that includes prison, or worse yet, cemetery visits.* Because of me, Blake's future would now be filled with cemetery visits.

"If...if I don't make it out alive, please tell my husband and kids I love them."

I closed my eyes and allowed my tears to flow. I'd done everything I could to help myself. Either the police would come to my rescue, or they wouldn't. I forced myself not to think about what might happen if no one had been listening in on the other end of my cell phone. Instead, I focused on happier times and clung to the possibility of rescue.

Rudy had not allowed me to grab a jacket before forcing me from my home. Even though autumn had arrived only days ago, the mercury had recently nosedived. A cold, damp wind blew outside, rattling the wooden siding of the old garage and brushing tree limbs against the hole-riddled roof. The chill crept into the Pathfinder and permeated my bones. If Rudy left me here all night, he wouldn't have to kill me. I'd freeze to death first. So much for trying to think happy thoughts.

I strained to hear outside noises—traffic whizzing down the street, leaves swirling in the wind, squirrels scampering overhead—hoping to hear the sounds of the cavalry charging to my rescue.

What I heard instead were footsteps crunching on leaves right outside the garage. Rudy had received his payment, and I was about to die.

TWENTY

But instead of Rudy coming to kill me, an angry voice, boomed from a loudspeaker. "Rudy Klingerhoff, you're surrounded. Come out with your hands up!"

Rudy apparently had other ideas. He responded with bullets. The gunshots echoed around me, quickly answered by a return volley. Then all hell broke loose. The Pathfinder reverberated from what sounded like hundreds of exploding firecrackers. The acrid smell of gunpowder filled the car, stinging my eyes and burning my lungs.

Bullets ripped through the garage, some hitting the Pathfinder. I had no idea whether I was caught in the crossfire or Rudy was trying to carry out his hit by exploding the car's gas tank. Either way, I didn't like the odds, and I had no way of improving them. I couldn't even duck.

I sandwiched my head between my arms and yelled at the top of my lungs, "Stop shooting at the garage!" Not that I expected anyone to hear me above the gunfire, but I refused to sit there passively accepting my fate.

A bullet shattered the back windshield and whizzed by, inches from my head, before exploding the front windshield. I screamed so loudly I think I ruptured my vocal chords.

Then as suddenly as the gunfire started, it stopped. I inhaled a grateful, albeit shaky, breath, waiting for release from my prison. But instead of hearing the sound of someone cutting through the chain on the door, an enormous explosion ripped through the air. The Pathfinder bounced side to side, nearly toppling before it righted itself, as the garage shifted off its foundation, splitting some of the support beams. Seconds later I saw flames licking at the roof and dancing down the sides of the wooden walls.

The garage quickly filled with dense black smoke that curled its way into the Pathfinder. Far worse than the smoke from the bullets, this was killer smoke, the kind that sucks the oxygen from the air—the kind where you're supposed to get down on the ground and crawl to safety to keep from dying of smoke inhalation. I began to cough, then wheeze, gasping for breath.

Within seconds I saw nothing but the shadow of the dashboard in front of me, but soon that, too, disappeared into the blackness. Over the roar of the flames I thought I heard shouting coming from beyond the garage. I tried shouting back, screaming at the top of my lungs, but no sound came out other than rattling wheezes as I fought to pull oxygen into my lungs. I yanked so hard at the handcuffs that they sliced into my wrists. I felt the blood drip down my arms at the same speed as the tears streaming down my cheeks. Violent spasms wracked my body until my lungs finally gave up the fight.

~*~

I came to strapped to a gurney inside a careening ambulance.

Sirens blared as I bounced and jostled, an oxygen mask covering my mouth, an IV tube snaking into my arm. Blake leaned over me. I'd never seen him so scared. I tried to raise my head but couldn't. "Lie still," he said. "You're going to be all right."

I closed my eyes again. They burned too much to keep them open. "She will, won't she?" I heard him ask someone, but I didn't hear a reply.

The next time I awoke, I found myself on a bed in a hospital room. Machines beeped and whirred around me. My lips curled around a large plastic tube. Another tube snaked into my left arm. Every part of my body ached, burned, stung, or throbbed. I embraced the pain; it meant I was alive.

"Gracie?" I turned my head to find Blake seated in a chair beside the bed. My eyes filled with tears as he gently laced his fingers between mine. He raised my hand, and I saw a bandage wrapping my wrist. "I thought I lost you," he said.

I smiled and squeezed his hand before I fell back to sleep. I continued to drift in and out of sleep for what was either hours or days. I had no concept of time. However, each time I awoke, I found Blake sitting beside me. I'd squeeze his hand, then drift off again.

Eventually, I remained awake long enough to learn I'd suffered smoke inhalation. The doctors had intubated and sedated me, which explained why I never stayed awake for very long. Thanks to the tube running down my throat, when I was awake, I couldn't speak. Panic over the unknown gripped me. Was this permanent?

Sensing my anxiety, Blake reassured me that the tube was temporary. However, grief and fear had etched deep lines into his face, and I didn't know if he was being truthful or just trying to keep me calm.

Once the doctors began weaning me from the respirator, while also decreasing the sedatives and painkillers, I remained awake for longer periods of time. When the fog lifted from my brain, I pantomimed for a pencil and paper. *You should be enjoying the reprieve from my constant babbling* I wrote.

Instead of giving me *The Look*, as I had expected, Blake's eyes filled with tears. That's when I realized the seriousness of the situation. *Trying to cheer you up* I quickly wrote, adding a smiley face.

He forced a smile. "I miss your babbling."

I had a million questions that demanded answers. *Is Rudy behind bars?*

"He's dead."

How?

"The police aren't sure. The house exploded. Rudy had an arsenal stored inside. No one knows if he blew himself up, or one of the S.W.A.T. team bullets triggered an explosion. Either way, you don't have to worry about him anymore."

He seemed like such a nice guy.

"That's what you said about Sidney Mandelbaum, and he turned out to be a con artist."

I shook my head. I never thought Not-Sid was a nice guy. I put up with the creep because I wanted his Mandelbaum Moolah. I'd just never let on to Blake the extent of Not-Sid's creepiness. Maybe it was time to come clean.

"Which reminds me," said Blake. "The police did take DNA samples from Blanche Becker's sons. The results came back positive. Blanche was right all along. Sidney was Sheldon Becker. The *Star-Ledger* ran a front-page story yesterday. I saved it for you."

Not-Sid wasn't all that nice. I just never told you.

Blake scowled. "I figured as much. What else did you hide from me, Gracie?"

I shook my head. *Rudy was different. He seemed so lonely and sad. Vulnerable.*

"Sociopathic."

I nodded. I'd come to the same conclusion during my ordeal. *What about Leila and the other women?*

"According to Detective Menendez, Suzette, Maureen, and Mary Louise ratted Leila out, hoping by turning on her they'd receive suspended sentences. Leila tried to cut a deal, but with Rudy dead, she had nothing to offer."

What about her family connections?

"Apparently, she wasn't connected enough to interest the prosecutor."

They're all in jail? For how long?

"A very long time. Even though all four pleaded guilty, the sentencing judge wasn't in a very generous mood. Unless they live to see their hundredth birthdays, they'll each spend the remainder of their retirements in orange jumpsuits. You're safe, Gracie. You have nothing more to worry about."

Except for the prospect of living above an auto repair shop in Newark. Unless...*Can we file civil suits against Leila, Suzette, Mary Louise, and Maureen?* Those women should pay huge bucks for what they'd put me through.

"We could, but we wouldn't get much."

Not even from Leila and Mary Louise? That made no sense. Judging from their homes, those two were loaded.

"All four women were living well beyond their means, mortgaged to the hilt with huge credit card debt. That's why they were each interested in Sidney—or Sheldon—at first. They wanted to marry him for his money."

Talk about irony! *The con man was being conned?*

"Separately by all four. At some point one of them must have mentioned she'd hooked a wealthy guy, and they realized they were all dating the same man. That's when they hatched a plot to get even."

A plot that backfired on them and nearly cost me my life.

The apartment above the auto repair shop was back in our future. I could safely assume Blake would force me to fold Relatively Speaking. Not that I had any desire to continue playing wing woman to single seniors. I'd learned my lesson. I was steering clear of all septuagenarians from now on—at least until Blake became one. Relatively Speaking was officially permanently dead.

The demise of my fledging business would make Blake extremely happy. He probably wouldn't even mind that apartment above the auto repair shop in Newark. I wasn't as accepting. Now, more than ever, I needed to become a bestselling romance author. Only one obstacle stood in my way—I had to finish the damn book.

A NOTE FROM THE AUTHOR

Dear Reader,

I hope you enjoyed *Definitely Dead*, the first book in my Empty Nest Mystery series. If so, please consider leaving a review at your favorite review site.

Gracie really did write a romantic comedy called *Hooking Mr. Right*. (Well, actually I did under my Emma Carlyle pen name.) If you're a mystery reader who also enjoys reading romantic comedy, buy links for *Hooking Mr. Right* can be found on my website at www.loiswinston.com.

Happy reading!
Lois Winston

ABOUT THE AUTHOR

USA Today and Amazon bestselling and award-winning author Lois Winston writes mystery, romance, romantic suspense, chick lit, women's fiction, children's chapter books, and nonfiction under her own name and her Emma Carlyle pen name. *Kirkus Reviews* dubbed her critically acclaimed Anastasia Pollack Crafting Mystery series, "North Jersey's more mature answer to Stephanie Plum." In addition, Lois is an award-winning craft and needlework designer who often draws much of her source material for both her characters and plots from her experiences in the crafts industry. Learn more about Lois and her books, where to find her on social media, and a link for signing up for her newsletter at www.loiswinston.com.

Made in the USA
Monee, IL
08 December 2022

20033150R00132